ENTICING THE EARL

The Arrogant Earls
Book Three

Kathleen Ayers

ARE YOU SIGNED UP FOR DRAGONBLADE'S BLOG?

You'll get the latest news and information on exclusive giveaways, exclusive excerpts, coming releases, sales, free books, cover reveals and more.

Check out our complete list of authors, too!

No spam, no junk. That's a promise!

Sign Up Here

www.dragonbladepublishing.com

Dearest Reader;

Thank you for your support of a small press. At Dragonblade Publishing, we strive to bring you the highest quality Historical Romance from some of the best authors in the business. Without your support, there is no 'us', so we sincerely hope you adore these stories and find some new favorite authors along the way.

Happy Reading!

CEO, Dragonblade Publishing

Additional Dragonblade books by Author Kathleen Ayers

The Arrogant Earls Series
Forgetting the Earl (Book 1)
Chasing the Earl (Book 2)
Enticing the Earl (Book 3)

CHAPTER ONE

London, 1842

"MRS. HONEYWELL."

Oleana sneezed. Scratched at her nose. Stretched her fingers in the direction of her quarry. Just another inch or so. Her entire body save the backs of her legs was beneath the bed. She was sure her skirts had ridden up to reveal her ankles. A scandalous display that was yet another sign of her unsuitability for her current position.

The clearing of a throat sounded behind her. Annoyance reached Oleana even under a thick feather mattress. "Mrs. Honeywell."

Oh. Yes. Right. I'm Mrs. Honeywell.

"What is it, Wilbert?" She addressed the Earl of Monteith's butler, her words muffled by dust and four-poster bed.

"There's been another incident." Disdain dripped from his words.

Oleana kept her eyes focused on the dark depths beneath the bed and the task at hand. Grabbing Miss Straw's leg, she pulled hard as the butler's words sunk in.

Oh dear. An incident.

She inhaled a cloud of dust and sneezed again. Perhaps she should assign a maid or two to clean under the beds in the guest rooms. It was what a well-trained housekeeper in the employ of an earl would do. Unfortunately, though Oleana was Lord

Montieth's housekeeper, she wasn't really trained to manage the staff. Or work in tandem with a smug, self-important butler. All her experience had been as a vicar's wife, one whose main task had been sitting in a pew in the front row of the church, nodding politely when required, and tending to the necessities of her husband's flock. A task that had usually consisted of visiting sick villagers and delivering bread. Which she hadn't baked. The vicarage *had* a housekeeper, whose duties also extended into the kitchen. Oleana tried mightily to remember the tasks Mrs. Bellweather performed, but all she could recall was dusting and placing delicious meals on the table.

She pulled out the troublesome Miss Straw, grasping the doll triumphantly in one hand, and promptly hit her head on the sturdy walnut of the bed's frame. "Blast."

"You are a disaster," Wilbert hissed. "One can only hope such an injury will knock some sense into you, Mrs. Honeywell. Or perhaps remind you of your duties. I am hopeful you will soon disappear from whence you came."

Oleana took in the priggish butler. "Lady Elizabeth's doll was missing."

"Oh yes. I keep forgetting you've managed to insinuate yourself with Lord Montieth's daughter, causing the dismissal of Miss Abercrombie." Wilbert leaned over. "Mark my words, Mrs. Honeywell: the truth will yet come to light."

She pushed herself up from the floor, rubbing her head. "If you will recall, Mr. Wilbert, I asked Lord Montieth to please keep Lady Elizabeth's governess, as I am merely a housekeeper." Guilt had propelled Oleana to recommend Miss Abercrombie be kept on, for she had felt terrible someone might lose their position because of her. But it was clear to everyone, especially Lord Montieth, that his daughter had a marked preference for Oleana and hadn't cared for her governess.

Oleana didn't blame Elizabeth. Miss Abercrombie's sharp edges and harsh manner weren't the least appealing to a child of six with a curious mind.

Wilbert sniffed. "You are inepter at being a governess or nursemaid than a housekeeper."

Truthfully, she was qualified for none of those positions, of course. But what she did possess was honest, genuine affection for her employer's daughter.

And an unexpected, *unwelcome* attraction for Elizabeth's father, Lord Montieth.

"My methods might not be as structured as Miss Abercrombie's—"

Wilbert waved away her protests, peering down his slender, hooklike nose, scalding her with his dislike. "Your presence has been requested in Lord Montieth's study." A smug, toothy smile pulled at his thin lips. "Immediately."

Oleana turned from Wilbert's hopefulness she'd be sacked to Miss Straw. The porcelain doll had gone missing days ago, dragged away to be tortured, no doubt. Tiny claw marks decorated the exquisitely tailored velvet dress. The sash around Miss Straw's waist had been shredded. The doll's ash-blonde hair looked to have been gnawed on. Oleana may have to cut out some of the worst knots and restyle the strands into something more suitable.

Oh dear.

"I'll be along in a moment, Wilbert." She stood, doll clutched in one hand, and smoothed down the plain gray wool of her skirts. "You needn't wait."

"I'm to escort you."

He'd probably asked the earl for permission to do so. Wilbert would have made an excellent guard at a jail. Or perhaps an executioner. He so enjoyed the punishment of others.

The butler had disliked Oleana from the moment she'd knocked on the Earl of Montieth's door, a recommendation from the earl's elderly aunt clutched in one hand. Before Wilbert could toss her out, Oleana had started blathering away about Miss Symon. Miss Symon's fondest wish, Oleana had declared, was for her cherished housekeeper to find a position in London with her great-nephew, Lord Montieth. She'd stubbornly put one foot inside the door when Wilbert had tried to slam it shut in her face. He'd nearly taken her toes off.

But Oleana, desperate and determined, would not be put off.

After forcing herself inside Montieth's home, she'd repeated to Mr. Wilbert her well-rehearsed tale of an elderly woman whispering out her last wishes on her deathbed. Oleana had dangled the letter of recommendation from her fingers, Miss Symon's signature clearly visible, as the maids and two of the footmen had watched in stunned silence at the challenge to Wilbert.

Mr. Wilbert. Butler *and* petty tyrant.

Unable to throw her out now, not with witnesses who had seen the letter and heard the name of Miss Symon invoked, Wilbert had been forced to read the piece of paper. His eyes scanning the document, the lines around his mouth deepening with every word he read, Wilbert had snarled at Oleana to wait while he went to consult with Lord Montieth.

Now Oleana was a housekeeper. An incredibly poor one. The tasks assigned to her had been light, given Wilbert already ran the household with efficiency. Her duties were nearly nonexistent and mainly consisted of walking about the large house with a set of keys dangling from her waist, and attempting to look important. Taking on the role as companion to Lady Elizabeth had been no hardship nor had it taken Oleana away from anything of importance. She still couldn't find the main linen closet, the location of which changed depending on whom Oleana asked.

"Ticktock, Mrs. Honeywell. Lord Montieth does not care to be kept waiting."

Brushing past the self-important butler, Oleana promptly stumbled into the doorframe, ignored Wilbert's snort at her clumsiness, and strode from the room with as much pride as she could manage. At least she didn't trip on her own skirts again as she had the other day in front of one of the maids.

Carrying Miss Straw, Oleana made her way to Montieth's

study, the butler so close behind her she could feel his breath on the back of her neck.

She swallowed down the mounting trepidation at having to face her employer. The upcoming conversation was bound to be unpleasant. Every discussion with Lord Montieth since her arrival had been of a frigid nature. Montieth was the sort of lord who considered himself vastly superior to nearly everyone else, as his ancient and much-lauded title dictated. He was quite tall. Broad of shoulder and lean of form. He loomed over Oleana, often shooting annoyed looks down at her from his greater height.

Her insides twisted pleasurably. Annoyed or not, Montieth possessed the most beautiful eyes. Like slightly tarnished silver waiting to be polished.

Stop mooning over him.

The earl might well sack her over this latest incident, which would force Oleana to plead for her position. She had nowhere else to go at present, and there was safety to be had in the Earl of Montieth's household.

Pasting what she hoped was a contrite look on her face, she waited as Wilbert knocked on the door with a sharp rap of his knuckles.

"Come," a deep voice rumbled from within.

Annoyed. Monteith's usual tone when dealing with her or any of the other household staff. He always sounded as if something had soured in his mouth.

Such a lovely mouth.

Oleana pushed the thought aside. Montieth was also arrogant. Intimidating. Cold. She had yet to see his lips twist into anything other than a scowl. The fact he didn't like her in the least was largely her fault. And quite a shame because she really was quite likable, despite Wilbert's opinion.

Wilbert swung open the door at the earl's instructions, ushering Oleana inside with a little nudge at her back. The butler remained standing beside the door, determined to watch her humiliation.

Oleana clutched Miss Straw tighter, shifting to hide the doll in her skirts. It was difficult to maintain one's sense of professionalism with a half-chewed doll hanging from one's fingers.

"That will be all, Wilbert," Montieth said pointedly from behind his enormous desk without raising his gaze from the papers strewn across the top.

The butler's mouth stiffened further, lips twitching as he struggled to hide his disappointment at being dismissed from the dressing down Oleana was about to receive. "Should I take the liberty of having Mrs. Honeywell's things collected, my lord?"

Oleana inhaled sharply. *Presumptuous old codger.*

"I said that will be all, Wilbert."

Bowing, Wilbert cast Oleana a look of utter loathing before finally retreating.

She waited for Montieth's command to approach his desk, telling herself to remain perfectly still. Oleana took in the heavy dark wood of Montieth's desk, devoid of any ornamentation. Hideous. More appropriate for interrogating heretics during the Spanish Inquisition than sitting in an earl's study. She could well imagine Montieth as one of those terrifying inquisitors. If he weren't so bloody handsome.

The rest of the room gave off the same austere, chilly ambiance.

Burgundy velvet, trimmed with gold, hung from every window, parted only enough to allow the weak sunlight to breech the interior of the room. Bookcases lined one wall, filled to overflowing. Once, while pretending to inspect the shelves for dust, Oleana had examined those bookcases, curious to see what sort of literature Montieth collected. Boredom had driven her away. Every tome focused on only one thing: battles and military strategy of the Romans and Greeks. Particularly the Spartans. She glanced up at the earl, who had still not bothered to acknowledge her.

Two uncomfortable-looking chairs with high backs were positioned before the monstrous desk. A visitor was meant to sit in one of those chairs, looked down upon by Montieth as he lorded over them at his pleasure, drumming his beautiful, elegant fingers against the desk.

One would never have known she'd once been married to a vicar given the nature of her thoughts concerning Montieth, most of which were incredibly improper.

Correspondence sat in neat stacks to the left of the earl, sorted by date, sender, and event. She knew the exact order because Montieth's secretary, Jones, one of two he employed, had failed to correctly alphabetize the middle pile and nearly been dismissed over the error.

Montieth was particular about his correspondence.

The pile at the far right of the desk, minuscule in comparison to the other two, held invitations to those events Montieth had agreed to grace with his austere presence.

Oleana waited, her grip on Miss Straw growing clammy. The only sound was the ticking of the giant ormolu clock sitting atop the mantel and the scratch of Montieth's pen. Finally, he deigned to address her.

"Mrs. Honeywell." Montieth's massive shoulders had been somewhat hunched as he wrote, but now he straightened. Leaning back in his chair—more a throne, she supposed—he pierced her with a frosty look.

"My lord." Oleana dipped, her eyes catching on the shining bits of orange fur caught on the now visible sleeve of Montieth's expensively tailored coat.

She clutched Miss Straw tighter for support.

Oleana willed her spiking pulse to calm as his glacial stare met hers. Despite Montieth's obvious displeasure, all directed at her, her heart fluttered about wildly inside her chest at being so near him. A far-too-common occurrence. Though he possessed the personality of an icicle in the dead of winter and rarely smiled, Montieth's physical appearance reminded Oleana of a prince's in one of the fairy tales she'd read as a child. Strong jaw. Chiseled cheekbones. Full, far-too-sensual lips. Thick dark hair that, though clipped close to his head, still curled at the edges. He even smelled wonderful, pine and leather with a touch of spice. Sometimes she imagined him brandishing a sword and sitting atop a white horse, about to rescue a princess, which of course was Oleana.

"Sit, Mrs. Honeywell." A broad hand motioned to one of the horrid chairs.

Oleana made her way over and sat, crossing her ankles before placing Miss Straw on her lap. The sparse cushion beneath her didn't possess enough padding to blunt the feel of the hard wood. Wiggling about, she tried to find a comfortable position, a nearly impossible task.

Montieth cleared his throat. Loudly. "Mrs. Honeywell, is there a problem with your chair?"

"No, my lord." The puff of orange fur on his sleeve glared at her. He was either unaware of the state of his coat, *highly* unlikely, or he planned to use the tuft of orange to make his point before having her dismissed.

Far more probable.

"We had an agreement when I offered you a position, did we not, Mrs. Honeywell?" The timbre of his voice was deceptively gentle. Almost as if he was speaking to a lover.

A small shiver traveled down her spine. "We did, my lord."

The silver of his eyes flickered over the doll in her lap. "I didn't know my daughter's favorite doll would be joining us. Miss Straw looks a bit"—a slight twitch of his lips—"bedraggled."

"Apologies, my lord. Lady Elizabeth misplaced Miss Straw. I had only just found her when I was requested to attend you in your study. I haven't yet had time to return her."

A slight incline of his perfectly chiseled chin.

Really, why must he be so attractive? Seems such a waste given his demeanor.

"I made several concessions when I agreed to your employment, Mrs. Honeywell." Montieth paused for effect. "Compromises I was loath to make and am rapidly coming to regret. Nevertheless, your...*associate* seems anxious to jeopardize your position."

"I apologize, my lord."

"You are often apologizing, Mrs. Honeywell, yet my household continues to suffer."

Suffer was rather a strong word.

"Yes, my lord." She drew Miss Straw up in her lap as a sort of shield. If he was going to throw her out, Oleana dearly wished he'd hurry things along. She was already composing her plea for clemency.

The frosty glance ran over her, sparking bits of light against her skin, though nothing, not even anger, shone in his eyes. The silver orbs remained flat and devoid of emotion. If Montieth knew his effect on her, he gave no indication. Arrogance dripped off the edges of his broad shoulders, across the stretch of his chest and the long lengths of his legs.

His well-muscled legs.

Oleana hastily looked down at her lap. What on earth was wrong with her?

"I realize you made a deathbed promise to my great-aunt concerning the...beast," he continued. "A laudable vow. And I respect her wishes to a point. But—"

A streak of orange tumbled off the bookshelf and across the room, interrupting Montieth's speech. Something, probably expensive and irreplaceable, crashed to the floor. An entire row of thick tomes on the Peloponnesian War thumped against the rug, books spilling open, their pages exposed.

Montieth's mouth, so oddly sensual for such a cold man, pursed in annoyance.

Carrot, the large orange ball of fur that had lately become the bane of Oleana's existence, shot across the room, intent on wreaking havoc in Montieth's study. The cat paused, gave a feline roar, and leaped up the side of Montieth's chair.

Oleana winced at the sound of claws sinking into the expensive leather.

Carrot, uncaring of whether his presence was wanted, promptly settled atop the edge of the chair, teetering ever so slightly as he tried to regain his balance. One paw stretched over the earl's shoulder as the big cat began to purr loudly in her employer's ear.

Monteith raised a brow in Oleana's direction, irritation rolling off him in waves, but he didn't flinch. Not even when Carrot's tail batted his ear.

Oleana bit her lip, struggling not to laugh. This was an altogether dire situation.

"*This* is unacceptable, Mrs. Honeywell."

It really was. Carrot was hugely spoiled. Arrogant in a way only a cat could be. He did as he pleased, whenever he pleased. He was very much like the Earl of Montieth in that regard.

Oleana sat up and placed Miss Straw on the chair, meaning to march around the desk and take Carrot from Montieth's shoulder.

Montieth hissed in annoyance as Carrot's nose nuzzled his hair.

Oh goodness.

"He—likes you, my lord," she stuttered needlessly. "I've no idea why." Warmth flooded her cheeks. "What I mean to say is—"

Montieth held up a hand. "Not another word. Get this beast off me and keep him out of my study, Mrs. Honeywell. I don't want to see him, hear him, or find so much as a strand of orange anywhere on my person."

"Yes, my lord."

"If he so much as purrs in my ear, you will *both* be packed up and sent forthwith back to Shropshire, no matter the deathbed wishes of my great-aunt. Is that clear?"

Oleana made her way around the desk. Carefully picking up Carrot, she cringed at hearing the snag of threads as one of his claws refused to let go of the earl's coat.

"Carrot," she whispered. "Bad cat."

It was difficult to wrestle Carrot away from Montieth. The

cat was heavy. Fat, really. A large orange object that didn't wish to be moved.

Her hip bumped into the corner of the desk, and she stubbed her toe.

Montieth gave a sigh. Her clumsiness was one more thing that annoyed Montieth. Honestly, given how badly she and Carrot irritated the earl, it was a wonder she'd lasted this long in his household. If it weren't for Lady Elizabeth, Oleana would probably be sleeping in the street.

Her breast pushed against the earl's shoulder, nipple tightening to a small peak at the brush against the muscles beneath his coat.

Montieth's body grew taut. "He is barely feline," he snapped in an icy tone. "So overfed he rolls about rather than pounces. He should be living in the stables, attempting to earn his keep, though I doubt with his girth he has any chance at catching a mouse. I watched him chase a bird outside the window one day. A pathetic display of athleticism."

"Carrot is very old," she said in the cat's defense. "He means no disrespect."

"He's a menace, Mrs. Honeywell."

Carrot wasn't the least menacing unless you were Miss Straw. The cat was very fixated on Lady Elizabeth's porcelain doll just as he was Montieth. Neither returned his affections. Oleana sunk her fingers into Carrot's fur, her grip tightening around the struggling cat.

JASON SYMON, EARL of Monteith, tried without much luck not to stare outright at his housekeeper, or rather at the small dangle of copper curls hovering beneath one of her ears.

He did so love the color. Like a fiery sunset. Or leaves in autumn.

The strands sparkled in the sunlight filtering across his desk, making his fingers twitch with the urge to unleash all that flame and feel those curls spill over his hands. When her breast had accidentally pushed into his shoulder mere moments ago, Jason had nearly come out of his chair. His attraction for this small slip of a woman who was the poorest, clumsiest, least subservient housekeeper any gentleman of his standing had ever employed continued to grow no matter how he struggled to tamp it down.

The giant mass of fur named Carrot was the least of his concerns.

Pressing his fingertips into the curve of his desk, Jason willed a splinter from the well-polished wood to pierce his skin. Anything to stop the constant stream of carnal thoughts about his housekeeper as she struggled to pull the obese cat from his shoulder.

Mrs. Honeywell represented a particular sort of torture.

Jason did *not* seduce the staff. It went against every honorable bone in his body. But almost from the moment Mrs. Honeywell had set foot in his house, tripping over the edge of every rug, knocking assorted knickknacks off nearly every table in his home, terrible feline following in her wake, Jason had been...*overcome*. He was surrounded by the most beautiful ladies in the *ton* on any given evening, yet only this annoying woman aroused him to such an overwhelming degree.

His cock had hardened the moment Mrs. Honeywell had shoved her letter of recommendation beneath his nose.

Jason hadn't even needed a bloody housekeeper, especially one he imagined naked every time he saw her. But his aunt's letter, more a plea for Mrs. Honeywell's employment than a recommendation, had given Jason pause. As had all that flaming copper hair.

His fingers drummed loudly on the desk.

Great-Aunt Agatha, God rest her soul, had been a recluse until her death at the esteemed age of ninety-one early last year. His aunt *had* lived in Shropshire, just outside a tiny village with the unlikely name of Badger. Mrs. Honeywell's descriptions of his aunt's home matched Jason's memories, but if he recalled correctly, Aunt Agatha's household had been small, most of her servants as ancient as their employer. The chances his aunt had hired a stunning redhead as her housekeeper were so slim as to be impossible. Still, Jason hadn't visited Aunt Agatha for several years before her death. Things might have changed.

And Mrs. Honeywell possessed the most magnificent hair.

Her outlandish tale of working for his aunt *could* be true, in which case Jason felt obligated to retain her services. However, it had become clear since her arrival that Mrs. Honeywell hadn't a clue what was required of a housekeeper. Wilbert had already requested her dismissal several times. Jason had actually considered doing just that, despite his attraction to her or because of it, but then he'd become aware of his daughter's marked preference for Mrs. Honeywell over that of her governess, Miss Abercrombie.

Jason already hadn't cared for Miss Abercrombie, the fourth in a line of companions for his daughter. The woman had instructed the six-year-old Elizabeth to address him as Lord Montieth, not Papa. More unacceptable, Miss Abercrombie had informed Elizabeth of her lack of importance because she hadn't been born a male and therefore an heir. Jason had been furious.

Pushing aside such unpleasantness, he turned his attention back to Mrs. Honeywell. She stood before him, chin lifted mulishly, struggling to contain her savage beast of a cat while waiting for him to send her from the room. The light caught in her copper curls.

Damn.

His fingers drummed once more, disturbing the stack of invitations he had no intention of accepting. If he had to attend one more musicale in which a matron showcased her daughter's limited abilities on the harpsichord or piano, Jason might start screaming into his brandy. Playing an instrument wasn't enough of a qualification, in his mind, for a suitable wife.

Mrs. Honeywell cleared her throat. Carrot started to purr loudly.

Elizabeth was attached to both the cat and the housekeeper. She would be distraught to lose either. Mrs. Honeywell insisted Aunt Agatha had bestowed the care of the cat to her while his aunt had lain on her deathbed. A final request of sorts.

The story was complete rubbish. Aunt Agatha detested animals, especially cats. He'd recalled that pertinent fact just the other day while pushing the obese ball of fluff out of the study with the toe of his boot. Mrs. Honeywell wasn't telling the truth about having worked for Aunt Agatha, or at least not the entire truth. He was curious as to why.

He slid his hand down his thigh, fingers stretching next to his twitching cock.

Bloody hell.

Mrs. Honeywell's skin, Jason noted, had the sheen of cultured pearls. He longed to nibble along the column of her neck and drag his teeth over the satin of her skin. A vague floral scent clung to her as if she'd been rolling about naked in a field of wildflowers with all that stunning hair curling around her body.

His cock twitched again. Painfully.

Jason searched for something else to say, another reprimand or comment to keep her from leaving. It was really inexcusable, the lust he had for Mrs. Honeywell.

She cleared her throat again. "If that is all, my lord, I have duties to attend to."

He plucked off the small bit of orange fur from his coat and made a great show of dropping it slowly to his desk.

A frown crossed her lips. Her eyes, a clear, resolute blue, flashed defiantly in his direction before her features once more smoothed out into complete blandness.

Arousal stirred in him once more. No housekeeper worth her salt would have fixed her gaze on her employer in such a way. Wilbert, stuffed shirt that he was, had been correct on that point. Mrs. Honeywell lacked the manner of anyone who had spent their life in service. Which again begged the question of why she was masquerading as a housekeeper.

"Not quite, Mrs. Honeywell. Should I find Carrot in my study again, or my wardrobe—"

A squeak came from her plump lips. He wanted desperately to nibble at the bottom one. "Your wardrobe, my lord?"

"My valet found Carrot cleaning himself on a pile of freshly laundered shirts, Mrs. Honeywell. *My* shirts." There were also claw marks on the posts of his bed, but Jason made no mention of them.

"I see." The creamy skin flushed a deeper pink.

"My daughter's fondness for this creature"—he waved at Carrot—"and yourself will not be enough to save either one of you from banishment should I find *it*"—his voice rose an octave—"on my bed again."

Mrs. Honeywell, he didn't bother to add, would be welcome should *she* be found lounging across his pillows.

"Am I making myself clear, Mrs. Honeywell? Do you understand what is required to continue in your position within my household? Which is more companion to my daughter than housekeeper, I'm given to understand."

"Exceptionally clear, my lord." Her eyes were the exact shade of bluebells. Angry bluebells.

"I sense there is more you would like to say. Perhaps offer some sort of defense for that lump of cat you hold in your arms?"

"Not at all, my lord." But he could see she was struggling not to speak her mind.

"If you take Elizabeth to the park, please ensure a footman and one of the grooms accompany you."

"Why not Wilbert for good measure?" A tiny bit of sarcasm bled into her response.

Ah, there it was. The crack in her meek behavior. His lips twitched, Jason ever closer to smiling outright in her presence. "I think he's busy counting the silver today. I understand you have neglected to do so."

Mrs. Honeywell's eyes narrowed, her lips pressing together into a line. She dipped ever so slightly, the weight of the enormous cat nearly causing her to topple over.

Jason forced his gaze back to his desk, effectively dismissing her. The swish of her skirts alerted him she was leaving, and he raised his head in time to see the twitch of her hips as she exited the study. He stared at the letter in front of him for several moments, contemplating his aunt's shaky handwriting. There was no indication of when Aunt Agatha had written such a heartfelt recommendation for Mrs. Honeywell. It could have been years ago.

Which would have made his housekeeper barely more than a child at the time.

"Good day, my lord." His secretary Mathers, the one he liked more than the other, appeared at the door Mrs. Honeywell had neglected to shut. Yet another irritating aspect of her character: the inability to quietly shut doors behind her.

Jason waved the young man in. "Come."

"My lord, I'm to remind you that Miss Langham will be in attendance at the Danvers ball," Mathers informed him.

He'd forgotten about the damned ball. And Miss Langham.

"I suppose Lady Trent requested you encourage me to reply to Lady Danvers that I'll be in attendance?"

Mathers colored slightly.

Jane Langham, daughter of a viscount, hadn't crossed Jason's mind at all in the fortnight since he'd last seen her. Not that there was anything amiss with Miss Langham—quite the opposite. She was attractive. Well bred. Docile. Her qualifications were nearly identical to those of his first wife, Alice.

Jason batted away the slight bit of revulsion at the thought of his deceased wife.

No, there was nothing wrong with Miss Langham, and she was likely very different from Alice. But there wasn't so much as a hint of red in Miss Langham's hair. Nor did Jason ever imagine what her hair would look like spread across his bed. Or how she would taste if he kissed her.

"I'm curious: does my mother pay you a salary as well, Mathers?"

"Lady Trent does not, my lord," his secretary replied in a solemn tone at the mention of Jason's mother. "I would refuse if she did."

"You would lose, Mathers. Lady Trent is nothing if not determined and single-minded in her purpose. Just now that purpose is to see me wed."

"Yes, my lord."

His mother had decided it was high time Jason find another wife. Alice had been dead for well over five years. An heir for Montieth was needed. To further her point, his mother had gone to great pains this season to fling every eligible young lady in Jason's direction.

"Please send word to Lady Trent that I will be in attendance as promised. No need for further reminders."

Mathers bowed and turned to go.

"I'm not finished, Mathers."

His secretary turned back to him, patiently awaiting instruction.

Jason liked that about Mathers. No incessant questions. No objections to doing anything he was asked. Mathers merely did his job extremely well, anticipating Jason's demands with ease and confidence. He might not want to be sent to Shropshire. But he would go.

"I have a project for you, Mathers. One that requires the utmost discretion."

"Of course, my lord." Mathers was a lean, spare young man who looked a great deal like any number of middle-class clerks that populated London. Brown hair. Brown eyes. Well spoken but not enough to draw any interest, which made him entirely suitable for what Jason had in mind.

"I need you to leave in the morning. For Shropshire."

CHAPTER TWO

"SUMMON THE CARRIAGE, if you would, Wilbert," Jason ordered.

The butler, standing at attention, immediately turned and waved at one of the young footmen. "A moment, my lord."

Jason came to the foot of the stairs, already dreading this evening. Yet another dull affair tonight. Dinner at Lady Burlington's. He was sure to be seated near at least one suitable female who would stare at her plate most of the evening rather than make intelligent conversation. Most young ladies found Jason far too intimidating to speak or do little else but fidget next to him. The only redeeming aspect of the entire night would be the food. Lady Burlington employed a most excellent cook.

"Wilbert, where is Lady Elizabeth?" Jason had gone to his daughter's room a short time ago to bid her good night and found her not in bed as he'd expected her to be.

His butler's mouth curled ever so slightly, as if he'd bitten into a lemon. "Lady Elizabeth is in the garden."

"The garden? At this hour?" It wasn't terribly late, but Elizabeth was only six.

"She is in the company of Mrs. Honeywell, my lord. I have one of the footmen standing guard on the terrace to ensure Lady Elizabeth's safety."

Wilbert always gave the impression he expected Mrs. Honeywell to take Elizabeth and run off with her. Regardless of her lack of qualifications as a housekeeper, Mrs. Honeywell excelled at caring for Elizabeth.

"I see. Are you sure a footman was necessary?"

"I thought it a wise precaution, my lord. I did try to dissuade Mrs. Honeywell from visiting the garden in the middle of the night, but she insisted. I did not want to upset Lady Elizabeth by addressing Mrs. Honeywell's insubordination."

Wilbert was prone to exaggeration. Mrs. Honeywell wasn't a soldier who'd challenged his commanding officer. "Perhaps I'll check on them myself before departing. I'll return shortly." He held up his hand so the butler wouldn't follow. "Your presence is not required."

"Yes, my lord."

Despite Jason's suspicions of Mrs. Honeywell, Elizabeth was happier than she had been in a very long time. Miss Abercrombie wasn't the only governess and companion Elizabeth had rejected after a short period. Every woman Jason had hired previously bore a long list of references. Stellar recommendations of their abilities with children. But not one of those women, not even the nursemaid who'd watched Elizabeth after Alice's death, had made his daughter smile the way his housekeeper did.

If Mrs. Honeywell was a charlatan of sorts, she was a well-intentioned one.

Jason made his way to the back of the house before nodding to the young footman standing guard just inside the doors leading to the garden. "James, can you direct me to Lady Elizabeth and Mrs. Honeywell?"

"Yes, my lord. They're just beyond the fountain." He pointed to the middle of the garden, where a large stone fountain rose. "Moon bathing."

Jason coughed, wondering if he heard the young footman correctly. "Moon bathing?"

The footman nodded. "Yes, my lord." He opened the door for Jason.

Stepping out on the terrace, Jason peered across the garden in the direction of the fountain. He could just make out two forms lying on their backs in the grass, hands outstretched beneath the light of the full moon.

Moon bathing indeed.

He jogged down the steps, pausing at the sound of their voices in the night breeze.

"I've always wondered what the moon feels like," Mrs. Honeywell said. "Is it squishy like a feather mattress? Or smooth like the pebbles beneath a stream?"

"Cheese, Ollie." Elizabeth giggled. "The moon is made of cheese."

"Highly doubtful," Mrs. Honeywell laughed back. "How in the world would all that cheese get up there in the night sky? Though if the moon were made of cheese, and I'll admit that is a delicious thought, what sort would you imagine?"

Elizabeth was quiet for a moment. "Cheddar, I expect."

"I've always thought a fine Cornish Brie." Mrs. Honeywell's fingers crawled toward Elizabeth, taking her hand. "But possibly that is because I adore Brie."

"Stilton," Jason interjected. Something in his chest constricted at listening to them talk about cheese in the moonlight and holding hands. "Do you suppose there are special cows capable of producing the milk required to make moon cheese?"

"My lord." Mrs. Honeywell sat up and released Elizabeth's hand. "How unexpected."

"I'm sure it is," he said a bit more sharply than intended.

Elizabeth popped up as well. "Hello, my lord."

Jason winced at hearing his daughter refer to him so formally. He knew plenty of gentlemen who had their entire families refer to them by their titles, but it always struck Jason as far too formal and incredibly self-important. He was Elizabeth's father and wanted her to address him as such. "What are you two about out here in the middle of the night besides debating what sort of cheese the moon could be made of?"

A low meow sounded from somewhere in the garden. The

shrub to Jason's left shook violently before stopping.

"Carrot is stalking a mouse." Elizabeth gave him a wide-eyed look. "While we moon bathe."

"I find that highly doubtful, moppet. I'm not sure Carrot is capable of stalking a mouse. Rolling over the poor rodent, perhaps. Or possibly terrifying a smaller creature with his huge orangeness."

Elizabeth smiled at him. "Ollie is teaching me the constellations." Her tongue tripped over the lengthy word. "Over there is Orion." His daughter pointed up at a cluster of stars. "And we *are* moon bathing. It is a respectable pastime."

Ollie. Short for Oleana, Mrs. Honeywell's Christian name. He should discourage Elizabeth from such familiarity, but he didn't have the heart to. She was fairly beaming at him.

"What exactly is a moon bath?" he asked.

"Something I did as a young girl, my lord." Mrs. Honeywell sounded not at all contrite for having been found lying on the ground in her employer's garden, moon bathing with his daughter. Nor did she make excuses for her behavior as a proper governess or housekeeper would have done.

"Vastly enjoyable." She turned her lovely face to him. "The only requirement is imagination." A dubious look crossed her features as she stood.

Moonlight created pale shadows around her petite form, highlighting the curves of her cheekbones and line of her neck. He was eminently aware of how breathtaking she was, standing before him, waiting for him to reprimand her. She expected him to do so, as if he was such a priggish snob he didn't remember what it was like to view the world with wonder.

"I don't lack imagination, Mrs. Honeywell. Only, I find it applied to better things than debating whether the moon is made of cheese."

"A pity, my lord." It was obvious from her tone she found him completely lacking in any sort of humor or creativity. Her opinion bothered Jason more than he cared to admit.

"An earl cannot afford such frivolous pursuits." He winced at hearing how self-important he sounded. How dull. When Jason was a child, before duty had been drilled into him and he'd inherited an earldom, he'd thought about the moon quite a bit. As well as the stars. Now he rarely considered either. Or the beauty of the night sky.

She made a small, disgruntled sound as if she thought he could do with a great deal more frivolity. Bending, she picked up the blanket, tickling Elizabeth as she did so.

"What do you see, Mrs. Honeywell?" he said. "Besides cheese?" Jason found his housekeeper to be such a curious creature. An odd combination of whimsy and intelligence along with a healthy dash of the mysterious. All of it, especially her affection for his daughter, made Jason want her more.

"Possibilities." A tiny smile crossed her delicious mouth.

Had Elizabeth not been standing between them, Jason was certain he would have kissed Mrs. Honeywell, right there in full view of one of the footmen. Probably Wilbert as well, because the butler was likely spying on them from inside the house. He wouldn't have been able to stop himself.

Another yowl echoed around the fountain.

Elizabeth looked up at Jason, her delicate features half-hidden in moonlight. She giggled softly. "Carrot has fallen on a mouse. Just as you said."

He reached down and picked her up, gratified when she snuggled against him. "Crushed the poor mouse beneath his orange stoutness. I venture he's rolling over him right now for good measure." Jason pressed a kiss to her temple. "Shall I take you up to bed and tuck you in before I leave?"

"Must I go up to bed, my lord?" She turned a beseeching look toward Mrs. Honeywell.

"Lord Montieth is correct. It is time for bed, Lady Elizabeth. Our duties to the garden will come very early." Mrs. Honeywell tucked the blanket beneath her arm.

The very last thing Jason wanted to do was leave the presence of Mrs. Honeywell or his daughter. A vision of the three of them, lying in a row while looking at the moon, nearly made him suggest doing such a ridiculous thing. Which annoyed Jason to no end. "Duties to the garden? Shouldn't Elizabeth be practicing her sums rather than digging in the dirt?"

Mrs. Honeywell turned her back to him, shoulders stiff, composing herself before she answered.

"My lord." Elizabeth's small fingers were wrapped around Jason's collar. "We have three rows of beans to tend. Each row has six plants. That is eighteen bean plants that require weeding."

Jason inhaled slowly. Numbers had proven difficult for Elizabeth. Miss Abercrombie had explained to Jason in her weekly reports on his daughter's progress that Elizabeth didn't have the mind for such expansive thoughts and implied Elizabeth lacked intelligence. Another thing he disagreed with Miss Abercrombie over. Perhaps it was only that Elizabeth hadn't had the proper instruction.

"That is quite a lot of beans." He pressed a kiss to his daughter's cheek and set her down. "Will you go up to where James is standing?" Jason pointed to the footman. "I want a word with Mrs. Honeywell."

"Don't trip over Carrot." She pointed in the direction of the fountain, where a round shadow lingered before disappearing again into the bushes.

"I won't. He's as large as a boulder and difficult to miss. Look, there's Bessie." He nodded to the young maid standing at the door. Bessie sometimes helped with Elizabeth. "Get ready for bed, and I'll be up directly."

"Good night, Ollie." Elizabeth waved at the slender form bathed in moonlight.

Mrs. Honeywell turned in Elizabeth's direction. "Good night, my lady. I'll see you first thing tomorrow," she said but made no move to come closer to him.

Jason watched her across the short distance that separated them, wondering why he found her so much more fascinating than Miss Langham.

"I am sorry, my lord, if I gave you any worry over Lady Elizabeth. That was not my intention. Wilbert was informed of our whereabouts. A footman was sent to watch over us."

"You were showing her the constellations."

"She has a keen mind, my lord."

"And teaching her how to do sums by using bean plants."

"Lady Elizabeth loves plants. I thought it might make more sense to her."

He hadn't known his daughter loved the garden. But Mrs. Honeywell did. "And moon bathing?"

A smile tugged at her lips. "You should try moon bathing sometime, my lord. You might like it."

Only if you are next to me.

Jason savagely pushed aside the thought, reminding himself that not only was Mrs. Honeywell in his employ—

And I do not tup the staff.

—but there was a very strong possibility she had lied to gain her position. Jason wasn't fond of deviousness in females no matter the cause. "See that Elizabeth is being instructed properly and not just in the course of moon baths, Mrs. Honeywell."

"Of course, my lord."

"Good night, Mrs. Honeywell." Jason went up the steps leading to the terrace. He was going to be late for Lady Burlington's dinner. Not that it would matter to his hostess. She'd been so thrilled he'd accepted her invitation that he could arrive while dessert was being served and she wouldn't so much as say a word.

He turned as he reached James, expecting Mrs. Honeywell to be behind him, but his housekeeper was still standing in the garden, her small form shining beneath a patch of moonlight, looking out over the garden.

A round shadow came out from beneath one of the trees close to the stone wall encircling his property and lumbered slowly in her direction. His housekeeper stooped and picked up the cat before turning back to the house. As Jason stepped back inside, he heard her mutter, "You'll get that mouse next time, Carrot. I know you will."

CHAPTER THREE

O LEANA'S HEELS CLICKED against the wood floors as she made her way past the library, searching for a splash of orange among the potted ferns standing guard at intervals in the hall. As fond of growing things as she was, Oleana's affections ran more to useful plants. Flowers. Vegetables. Herbs. Ferns, as far as she could tell, served no purpose other than to droop when requiring water.

Carrot, much to her dismay, had escaped once again, dashing from her room with a speed of which she hadn't thought him capable. He'd half run, half rolled away from Oleana before she could catch him. Since her last pointed reprimand involving Carrot, she had taken extra care to keep track of the large cat's whereabouts, and Carrot was confined to her room as much as possible. Which in turn helped Oleana avoid Lord Montieth.

Montieth seemed to inspire flippant answers in Oleana. She was far more concerned her tongue would cause her dismissal than she was Carrot would. The incident involving moon bathing had been a perfect example. Why hadn't she simply led Elizabeth inside when Monteith had appeared? Instead, she'd implied he lacked imagination and was dour, all while finding out he liked cheese, preferably Stilton. She'd been so aware of him standing in the garden like a perfectly carved, bloody beautiful statue that Oleana had found herself unsettled, which in turn had had her resorting to mild sarcasm to blunt the force of her attraction.

Yesterday, she'd caught sight of Montieth watching her and Elizabeth pluck weeds from the kitchen garden. They'd counted each weed and placed them in piles of five, which she'd then had Elizabeth add together. Her young charge loved plants. Gardens. Herbs and sunshine. She would wither were she to be trapped once more in the schoolroom. Oleana had held her breath as Elizabeth had patiently counted out the weeds, waiting for Montieth to come marching outside to chastise her for not instructing his daughter properly.

"I'm not even the bloody governess," she whispered.

Nor a housekeeper either. But that wasn't the point.

Oleana *was* educated. Far more than a moderately well-to-do farmer's daughter should be. But her father had once been a scholar of sorts, before he'd turned to farming, her mother the granddaughter of a baronet. Oleana's pedigree, poor as it was in comparison to someone of Montieth's standing, had barely made her acceptable to Mrs. Caraway.

She stopped, right in the middle of the hall, and took a deep breath.

Do not think of Mrs. Caraway.

Nodding to herself, she continued, pausing every so often, ears cocked, listening for any sign of Carrot. He was exceptionally loud for a cat, which usually made him easy to find.

"Carrot," she hissed. "Where are you?"

The low rumble of a purr echoed from further down the hall, coming from the direction of the drawing room.

Oleana said a silent prayer for divine intervention: *Please* don't let Carrot be in the drawing room, leaving orange fur all over the expensive damask-covered settee. Or eating the fringe off one of the decorative pillows. Or clawing at the tapestry depicting a bucolic scene some ancient Montieth had woven.

Thankfully, after a careful glance, Oleana could ascertain the doors to the drawing room were shut. A murmur of voices came from within, along with the delicate sound of a teacup and saucer. Monteith rarely entertained callers in the drawing room, preferring to use his study for business. The use of the room today could only mean the formidable Lady Trent, Monteith's mother, was visiting.

And Carrot was on the loose.

Oleana took a few quiet steps in the direction of the drawing room, peering underneath a long, rectangular table with slender legs. Atop the table sat a large urn. Probably Grecian. Maybe Egyptian. Oleana didn't exactly have an eye for such things.

"I'm thrilled you finally agreed to attend the Danvers ball." The rich, aristocratic voice clipped the air. "I grew concerned you might have overlooked the invitation."

Oleana winced at the sound of Lady Trent's imperious reprimand, almost feeling sorry for Lord Montieth. She had met his exacting mother once before, and neither party was enamored of the other.

"What an unfortunate shade of hair you possess, Mrs. Honeywell," Lady Trent had said. "Wilbert tells me your housekeeping skills aren't up to snuff."

"I didn't realize I had a choice, Mother," Montieth said. "Besides, you instructed Mathers to remind me."

"Who? Oh, you mean that lovely young man who does your bidding?"

"He's my secretary, as you well know."

"Then he is aware of your need for a wife to provide an heir, else he could find himself out of work. Perhaps Mathers took it upon himself to ensure you attended the ball as any good secretary would."

"I doubt Mathers cares, Mother, whether I court Miss Langham," Montieth drawled. "And I'm fairly certain his position is safe if I don't produce an heir in the immediate future. Did you put him up to it or not?"

"Very well. I asked Mathers to merely *suggest* you remember to attend." A frustrated sigh filled the air. "Really, Montieth. If you wish to find a bride, you've got to put in a bit more effort. I feel as if I'm doing all the work in sorting through the dozens of eligible young ladies this season. Your lack of interest is rather off-putting. Don't you want to remarry?"

"Of course I do."

"Then you must at least offer me some guidance. It isn't as if you're grieving over Alice. Not only has she been dead for some time, but the two of you could barely stand to be in the same room together. Especially after all the nonsense with Baron Lansing. She should have produced an heir before embarking on—"

"Enough, Mother. I don't care to discuss Alice or her cousin. Nor do I want Elizabeth to overhear you doing so. Alice's affairs were her own. I didn't care what she did with who; I only detested her lying about it. Honesty is something I value quite highly."

"Yes, well you certainly didn't get that from your sire."

Oleana backed slowly away from the door not wanting to be caught eavesdropping on what was a very private conversation. She hadn't known Montieth was in the market for a wife, though of course he had to be. He needed an heir. So, in addition to the sort of cheese Montieth liked, she now knew her employer put a high value on honesty. And the former Lady Montieth had been having an affair.

A tiny bit of dread pooled in her stomach at the thought of Montieth finding out Oleana's secrets.

"I thought you liked Miss Langham, darling." Lady Trent's voice softened.

Another purr echoed, as if Carrot was in a cave.

Oleana's eyes fell on the urn.

"I don't *dislike* her. But—"

Oleana could practically hear Montieth shrugging his deliciously broad shoulders.

An annoyed gasp came from Lady Trent. "Well, whether you do is irrelevant."

"Is it, Mother? Shouldn't I at least have a liking for her?"

"She's perfect for you. Exemplary pedigree. Modest to a fault.

Her family is respected, moderately wealthy. Even better, she has three sisters, all of whom produced sons within the first year of marriage. And she's hopelessly enamored. You could do far worse."

"I suppose I could," came Montieth's bored reply.

"Elizabeth needs a mother. A *proper* lady to guide her. I would offer to do so, but—"

"I wouldn't ask that of you, Mother. Besides, wouldn't your charity work suffer?"

"I suppose it would." Lady Trent sounded a little hurt at Montieth's quick dismissal. "You should never have tossed out Miss Abercrombie. She came with fine recommendations. As did the governesses you employed previously. I'm not sure what you found in them to be lacking." Silk rustled.

"Elizabeth detested Miss Abercrombie." Montieth's dislike of the former governess bled into his words, surprising Oleana. Wilbert always insisted Oleana was to blame for Miss Abercrombie's dismissal, but she could see he'd exaggerated. It was Montieth who hadn't liked the woman.

Another purr rippled around Oleana. Was Carrot trapped in the walls? *Impossible.* He was far too fat to accomplish squeezing himself into a crawl space, wasn't he?

"Carrot," she whispered, glancing again at the urn. The very tip of an orange tail popped out of the opening, flicking over the rim.

Oh. No.

Oleana made her way to the expensive-looking urn, her eyes on the drawing room doors, praying they would stay shut. There were at least a dozen vases, pots, and other bits of assorted, equally expensive objets d'art scattered throughout the hall, but of course Carrot had chosen *this* particular urn sitting outside the drawing room at the exact moment Lady Trent visited.

She stood on tiptoe and peered inside. "What is wrong with you?"

A glowing pair of green eyes looked back at her.

With one last glance at the drawing room doors, Oleana reached inside the urn for Carrot.

Carrot meowed in outrage at being disturbed. The table, far too fragile to hold an urn, especially one containing an overly large cat, wobbled. The ornate container tipped to the side.

Panicking the urn would fall to the floor and shatter, Oleana reached out with both arms, clasping the urn to her chest as Carrot peered at her through the opening. She stumbled, the hem of her skirts becoming trapped beneath her heel. As so often happened. Her clumsiness was rapidly becoming legendary in Montieth's home.

Drat.

She fell hard on her back, spreading her legs to keep from rolling to the side and breaking the urn, which was certainly a priceless heirloom. Carrot, the very worst cat in history, nonchalantly strolled out of the opening and climbed over Oleana's face, making sure to drag his tail over her mouth before leaping across the hall, wobbling slightly, and then disappearing.

Spitting Carrot's hair out of her mouth, Oleana lay sprawled in the hallway, legs askew, clutching the urn for dear life. Bits of orange fur floated in the air, announcing Carrot's retreat.

There were days she really hated that cat. Like today.

The doors to the drawing room flew open.

CHAPTER FOUR

"WHAT IN THE world—" Lady Trent gasped. "Good Lord." She made a great show of shielding her eyes from the horrifying display of Oleana and the urn spread out across the floor. "Get up this instant." Lady Trent shot an accusatory look over her shoulder at Montieth.

The earl stood behind Lady Trent, tall and imposing as ever, the smoky silver of his eyes focused solely on Oleana. Or more exactly, her legs. Possibly her underthings. Montieth was staring at her as if he wished to *devour* her. In slow, tiny bites with his sensual mouth.

Clearing her throat simply to dispel the heat tugging at her breasts and the apex of her thighs, she set the urn carefully to the side. Sitting up on her elbows, Oleana hastily tugged down her skirts.

The heated look from Montieth didn't dissipate in the least. She might well burst into flames if he didn't look away.

Lady Trent shook her head, fingers placed at her temple as if she might swoon in utter horror at the scene Oleana unintentionally presented. "This is what I speak of, Montieth. It is not a good example for Elizabeth to emulate. This—display is most unwelcome."

Oleana's lips tightened. It wasn't as if she'd fallen on purpose. And she was fully clothed, not scandalously displayed as Lady Trent's tone suggested.

"I apologize, my lord," she addressed Montieth. "I bumped into the table while on my way to the drawing room to see if you required anything," she lied smoothly. "I grabbed—"

A bit of orange fluff floating in the air settled on one of Oleana's breasts. She tried to brush it off before Montieth could see it.

The silver gaze followed the movement of her fingers as she plucked off the fur.

"I'm somewhat clumsy," she stammered as a slow, delicious curl of warmth wrapped around her midsection, pulsing out across her skin.

"An unwelcome trait in a housekeeper, clumsiness," Lady Trent snapped at Oleana before glaring at Montieth. "She could have broken that urn. It is *priceless*."

Oleana bit back the retort hovering on her tongue, difficult when she was so tempted to defend herself. True, the piece of pottery she had saved might be priceless, but it was overly ornate, somewhat lacking in taste, and could only be improved upon if it *were* broken.

The intensity faded from Montieth's handsome features, but his eyes still shimmered at her like bits of silver. Not a smile but certainly not a frown twitched at his lips as he regarded Oleana.

Another burst of warmth spread across her chest.

"Lord Montieth's father brought that urn back from a trip to Egypt," Lady Trent intoned in her self-important way. "I'm sure it once belonged to a pharaoh. Priceless."

"No, he didn't, Mother. The urn was purchased on Bond Street from an antiquities dealer. Even so, I doubt it is priceless or rare. The dealer in question came under suspicion later for peddling fakes."

"Nevertheless." Lady Trent gave Oleana an imperious look. "The urn decorates the home of an earl and is thus valuable. You would do well to be more careful, Mrs. Honeywell. This is not the home of a barrister or some merchant. Not even a vicar. This is the home of a *peer*. I find it impossible you've managed a household before, let alone one that belonged to our dear Agatha."

At the mention of a vicar, Oleana felt the blood drain from her face. She lowered her gaze away from Lady Trent and Montieth. Surely if either one knew who she really was, this conversation would be completely different.

"Well? Have you nothing to say, Mrs. Honeywell?" Lady Trent sniffed.

"Mrs. Honeywell is in my employ, Mother," Montieth interrupted. "Not yours. Much like Mathers works for me, not you. Stop ordering about my staff." Montieth approached Oleana, offering his hand to help her up. "No harm has been done, after all."

"Humph. My sensibilities have suffered." Lady Trent turned and retreated to the drawing room, in a flurry of skirts and rosewater.

Montieth pulled Oleana to her feet but didn't immediately release her fingers. "I sense Carrot's hand in this." The soft growl rippled over her skin. His gaze lingered slowly over the panicked rise and fall of her breasts. "The evidence is before me." He nodded to a bit of fur she'd missed.

Oleana's heart fluttered softly as the skin across her arms prickled at his nearness. For a moment, she thought he might pluck that bit of orange fur from her breast.

Part of her wished he would.

Montieth let go of her hand, far too slowly and a bit reluctantly.

An awkward silence filled the air, Oleana's awareness of Montieth so sharp she had to turn her back to him. She busied herself with setting the urn to rights on the table, pretending to swipe at a bit of dust. Finally, she said, "I don't know how Carrot got inside."

"A mystery. There seem to be many in my house," Montieth said quietly. His eyes caught hers once more before he returned to Lady Trent and the drawing room, shutting the door behind him.

Oleana let out the breath she'd been holding. It was dangerous to leave the safety of Lord Montieth's home, but after today, it might be just as dangerous for her to stay.

THE SIGHT OF Mrs. Honeywell's ankles had nearly undone him.

Ankles. Common enough. He'd seen dozens.

As Jason sat and listened to his mother drone on about the suitability of a variety of young ladies whose faces he couldn't recall, all he could think of was Mrs. Oleana Honeywell. The tiny copper curl, the one that taunted him at every turn, had slipped free in her efforts to save the urn, dangling just over one creamy cheek while she stared up at him.

How he longed to wrap the bit of copper around his thumb.

The curve of her knee. He wanted to press his mouth to the small hollow barely hinted at beneath her rucked-up skirts.

Jason had seen the panic in her face while his mother had chastised her over the urn, Mrs. Honeywell paling dramatically at the mention of Aunt Agatha. Or had it been over something else? Mrs. Honeywell clearly had secrets—ones Jason was determined to ferret out. Lately it had become his obsession, the mystery of Mrs. Honeywell.

"Montieth, are you even listening to me?"

"Of course I am. Miss Mary Duckworth is incredibly delightful." He pasted a dutiful look on his features.

His mother nodded before continuing to rattle on about Miss Duckworth. Jason's thoughts were still on his housekeeper.

And that tantalizing, tempting copper curl.

CHAPTER FIVE

"WOULD YOU CARE for more tea, Miss Straw?"
Oleana leaned over and pretended to fill the doll's teacup. "Sugar? Milk?" Nodding as if the doll had answered, she pretended to stir in a bit of sugar. "There you are, just as you like it, Miss Straw." Adjusting the flapping, broad-brimmed hat adorning her head, Oleana blew a puff of air at the stray fringe of ostrich feather that had fallen over her nose. The hat was an atrocity, covered with a ridiculous spray of ostrich feathers and cascade of moth-eaten ribbons. There was even a tiny fake bird missing a wing, perched on the rim. She wondered if the hat had once belonged to Lady Trent. Seemed like just the sort of overblown nonsense Montieth's mother would adore.

Oleana was still smarting from the grand lady's reprimand over the urn. She should be grateful Carrot departed before Montieth's mother could catch sight of him.

Elizabeth, sitting across from Oleana in the small room that had once been Elizabeth's nursery but now functioned more as a schoolroom or a perfect spot for tea parties, giggled before straightening her own hat. The blue velvet accessory was much too large for her young charge's head. The brim dipped low, nearly covering Elizabeth's eyes, and was decorated with a spray of grapes, an apple, and a pear.

Carrot meowed and stuck his nose into the saucer of milk and bits of chicken used to lure him to the tea party. He'd naturally refused a hat, though he'd gnawed on the ostrich feathers decorating Oleana's. Elizabeth had tied one of her father's cravats around Carrot's neck instead.

Elizabeth promised she'd been given the cravat by Montieth's valet, but Oleana wasn't so sure. She couldn't imagine Entwistle, the valet, who was far more pompous and self-important than Wilbert, parting with an expensive bit of silk to be used as a cravat for a cat.

As to the hats, Oleana had found them several weeks ago in the back of an old armoire while searching for Carrot. The armoire had been sitting forgotten in the far corner of a little-used guest room, reeking of neglect. Curious, and looking for Carrot as she often did, Oleana peered inside to see a great pile of hats, scarves, and bits of faded lace. The musty scent of lavender coming from the armoire was a sure sign no one had been interested in the contents for some time. There had been no sign of Carrot, but Elizabeth had been thrilled at the discovery. And the care of Montieth's daughter, as well as keeping Carrot out of trouble, seemed to be Oleana's primary duty these days. The household ran fine without her and always had.

Monteith didn't need a housekeeper, and he wouldn't need a companion for Elizabeth once he hired another governess.

Oleana bit her lip. She wasn't looking forward to leaving Elizabeth. Or Montieth.

"Will you pass the biscuits, Lady Ollie?" Elizabeth asked.

"Of course. What a poor hostess I am," Oleana said. "And you, Mr. Carrot?" She turned to the enormous tabby. "More milk?"

Carrot, exhausted from being chased down the hall by Oleana earlier and having to further endure the indignity of wearing Montieth's cravat, ignored her. Instead, he nibbled at a bit of chicken and eyed Miss Straw.

"Dolls are not on the menu today, Mr. Carrot," Oleana stated firmly.

"You cannot eat Miss Straw." Elizabeth laid her hand on

Carrot, who purred loudly at her touch. "I forbid you to." Her fingers curled into the orange fur. "Your affections, sir"—Elizabeth's tone took on a commanding edge, sounding remarkably like her grandmother Lady Trent's—"are not returned. The lady in question resents having her hair gnawed upon."

Oleana laughed, clapping her hands. "Well done, Lady Elizabeth. We cannot allow a gentleman's poor manners to go unnoticed. You are to be commended for bringing attention to his behavior."

Elizabeth grinned and took Oleana's hand.

Affection for Montieth's daughter bloomed fiercely within Oleana. It would pain her greatly when she had to leave Elizabeth, as she must do one day, and soon. The troubles from which she'd fled would not simply disappear, as much as she might wish them to. Mrs. Caraway would not give up so easily. But it would break Oleana's heart to leave Elizabeth.

On Oleana's second day at the earl's home, when she'd been exhausted at still not having located the elusive linen closet, she had walked outside into the garden for a breath of fresh air. A sob had met her ears, followed by a hiccup as Oleana had made her way toward a collection of peonies. Knowing peonies didn't usually sob to such a degree, she parted the branches of a small shrub and found Montieth's daughter.

My poor little darling.

Elizabeth, Miss Straw clutched in one hand, had wiped the tears from her eyes and claimed to be studying a caterpillar. Not weeping. And certainly not hiding from her governess, Miss Abercrombie.

Oleana had replied that she, too, was hiding, from Wilbert. She'd been rewarded with a shy smile from Elizabeth. Getting on her knees, Oleana had crawled into the bushes and studied the caterpillar, speaking gently to the upset child. It had taken some time before they were both in agreement the caterpillar was nothing more than a worm, and the conversation had evolved into a spirited discussion on ladybugs. Elizabeth had sought her out the following day. And the next. Soon Monteith's daughter had been actively evading her governess to spend time with Oleana.

Truthfully, Oleana couldn't have been happier. She adored Elizabeth. It was no hardship to be in her company. In fleeting moments, she could almost pretend Elizabeth was her daughter.

"Lady Ollie, another biscuit, if you please?" Elizabeth said.

Oleana held up the plate with a smile. "It would be my pleasure, though I must inform you, Lady Elizabeth, that too many might spoil your figure."

"Yes, I fear my corset is laced too tight as it is." Elizabeth gave Oleana an innocent look and then burst into giggles.

Oleana loved children. She'd hoped for at least a dozen of her own. The loss of those children that never were still pained her, but there was a reason, she supposed. Any child she would have conceived would have left her completely under the thumb of Mrs. Caraway forever. It was a blessing, though it didn't feel like one.

"Barren," her mother-in-law had whispered whenever she'd visited the vicarage. "Useless," she'd murmured as Oleana had poured her tea. Mrs. Caraway maintained that Oleana had been a poor choice altogether for a vicar's wife, with her flaming red hair and lack of humility.

Humility, as if Mrs. Caraway knew the meaning of the word.

At one point, Mrs. Caraway and Percival, her son and Oleana's husband, had made noises about securing an annulment due to her inability to conceive. Percival had grown resentful. Distant. He'd eyed Oleana more as a burden every day. Once, he'd been proud to show her off as his wife, but that had ended when she couldn't give him a child.

The Caraways had deemed her worthless—that was, until Mr. Hughes had arrived.

Fear, small but deadly, threaded through Oleana's stomach. Percival was gone, but his mother and stepbrother, Albert, were still very much alive. They had no idea she was in London. At least, not yet.

"Ollie, is that right?" Elizabeth asked.

"What, dearest?" She tucked a strand of Elizabeth's hair behind her ear, pushing aside the Caraways and the terrible fears thinking of them brought. She was safe for the time being. And Elizabeth needed her.

"We had ten biscuits when tea started," Elizabeth said. "Carrot hasn't had any. But I've eaten three, and there are six remaining." A tiny wrinkle creased her brow. "That is nine biscuits."

"So how many must I have eaten?"

"One. You've eaten one biscuit," Elizabeth crowed in triumph.

The first time Oleana had broached the topic of numbers, Elizabeth had burst into tears and claimed she was incapable of learning her sums. Miss Abercrombie had said she was quite hopeless and would be better off not bothering to learn at all. Thank goodness, the governess had informed Elizabeth, she was destined to be beautiful or else she'd never secure a husband.

Horrid, horrid woman.

Oleana had decided Elizabeth wasn't hopeless, only that Miss Abercrombie had been a poor teacher. Oleana had made a game of learning sums, using plants and seeds—two things of great interest to Elizabeth—instead of a chalkboard. Unsurprisingly, Elizabeth had begun to thrive. She was actually quite good at numbers when she had the incentive to learn and the proper encouragement.

"Correct, dearest. I'm so very proud of you." Oleana pressed a kiss to Elizabeth's cheek. "Well done."

Lady Trent would have a fit of apoplexy if she knew of Oleana's overfamiliarity with her granddaughter, but who else would see to Elizabeth's care? Lady Monteith had been dead before Elizabeth was out of the nursery, and though Oleana could see Monteith loved his daughter, it was also apparent he needed help. Elizabeth required a great deal of affection. Some children did.

Oleana had always thrived under her parents' attention as Elizabeth flourished under hers. Miss Abercrombie had certainly never shown an ounce of affection for her young charge, and Oleana doubted any of Elizabeth's former caretakers had taken the time to really know Montieth's daughter. It was a good thing he was searching for a wife, because Elizabeth needed a steady female influence in her life who was not Lady Trent.

According to the conversation she'd overheard between Montieth and his mother, it didn't seem he'd considered the former Lady Monteith to have been a good choice as a wife. Hopefully, Montieth would choose better this time. For Elizabeth's sake.

A painting of Lady Monteith hung in the hall downstairs, at the end of a long line of portraits of the earl's ancestors. Oleana had studied the pale, blue-eyed woman with the slightly upturned nose while pretending to dust the frame, trying to see Elizabeth in the woman's delicate features. Mrs. Beesom, the cook, had told Oleana that Lady Monteith had died from a fever after nursing her cousin, who had also perished. The frailty of Montieth's wife had been evident in the portrait, her skin so translucent Oleana had imagined she could see the delicate bones of her cheeks. A mass of flounces and lace from the extravagant gown she'd been painted in swallowed Lady Montieth's refined, slender form.

Montieth hadn't loved his wife; that much was clear. He didn't even seem to care she'd been involved with another man, only that she'd lied to him about it.

What would it be like to share a bed with Lord Montieth? A tingle shot straight down between Oleana's breasts at the thought.

Montieth was an attractive man in his prime. Based on his looks and title, Oleana doubted he was a stranger to feminine companionship even with his austere personality. He certainly could do far better than a housekeeper. Or a vicar's widow.

Her thoughts paused as she nodded at something Elizabeth was chattering away about.

Yes, she mused, he might have *momentarily* become undone by the sight of her ankles that day outside of the drawing room. Gentlemen often lost their wits at low necklines, glimpses of wrists, and the like. Ankles were no different, and hers were lovely. But she hadn't wisely fled her husband's family to stupidly enter into an indiscretion with her employer.

No matter how appealing the idea.

Mrs. Caraway often said Oleana possessed a lustful nature brought on by the shockingly obscene color of her hair, a wholly archaic and ridiculous observation. But perhaps there was a grain of truth to Mrs. Caraway's declaration. "Lustful" didn't begin to describe how Oleana felt about Montieth. It was much more than that. Akin to being devoured by flames.

Carrot stretched, one possessive paw landing on Miss Straw, purring loudly.

"Mr. Carrot." Oleana removed the cat's claws from the newly mended skirt of Miss Straw's dress. "You've such poor manners. Miss Straw has not welcomed your attentions. We will not be at home when you call next, sir, and your request for her hand is refused."

"Yes. Refused." Elizabeth burst into a fit of giggles while giving Carrot a stern glance.

"Poor Miss Straw, to have attracted a gentleman who licks his whiskers at tea," Oleana said in a prim tone. "She deserves so much better, does she not, Lady Elizabeth?"

"I quite agree." Elizabeth pushed the brim of her hat back.

Oleana's skin prickled softly in warning a second before the scent of pine and spicy shaving soap tickled her nostrils.

Carrot arched his back, tail flicking in anticipation.

"Good Lord," came a rumble from the doorway. "Is that one of my cravats?"

CHAPTER SIX

J ASON HAD SPENT the better part of the morning in his study, reviewing his ledgers. He had one property, Eastland, which was incredibly unprofitable no matter what changes were made. Eastland wasn't entailed. He should sell the estate and the land surrounding it, but Jason hated to admit defeat. Perhaps there was something else that could be done with the land. He made several notes for Jones, the secretary he didn't like as much as Mathers, who was still in Shropshire. Before he decided to sell Eastland, the property should be surveyed for coal and minerals.

Carriages passed by on the street outside his window. Two well-dressed ladies, maids following in their wake, strolled past. Beside his ledger sat a note from his mother, asking him to come for tea later in the week. Miss Langham and her mother would be in attendance.

Jason struggled to find anything other than apathy in the summons.

The Danvers ball had been everything Jason expected. Tedious. Dreadfully dull. Danvers hadn't even had a room set aside to play cards. The only thing that had injected the event with any amusement at all was the appearance of Lord and Lady Huntly. Hunt rarely attended social functions, mainly because he wasn't invited. But since deciding to court the former Emmagene Stitch and make her his countess, Hunt had developed a misguided sense of propriety. He wore clothing that actually fit well and made a concentrated effort not to spill wine on himself. He was often polite, so much so many thought him addled. Hunt had even made amends to Jason's mother, whom he'd offended over some trivial matter.

Hunt shouldn't have bothered. One could never completely pacify Lady Trent.

When Jason had spied Hunt, his massive form had been on the Danvers terrace, taking liberties with his own wife. Lady Huntly, not to be outdone, had been returning her husband's advances with great enthusiasm. Neither had so much as blushed when Jason had come upon them.

On the surface, the marriage of Miss Stitch, avowed spinster with a tongue so sharp most gentlemen found themselves sliced to ribbons with just a greeting, and the boorish, ill-mannered Earl of Huntly seemed a terrible mismatch. But Hunt and his wife were deeply in love. As was Jason's closest friend, Gideon, Lord Southwell, who had also wed.

Ironic given neither Hunt nor South had ever wished to be married.

Jason's first thought at the Danvers ball, other than how he might escape Miss Langham's company during their lone dance, had been that he *liked* the idea of taking liberties with his own wife. As Miss Langham had rattled on about a dinner party she'd attended, describing the event in detail, Jason's thoughts had been on the happiness of his friends. He was surprised to find himself envious. The idea of stealing a kiss from Miss Langham, should they wed, or groping her on a terrace while a ball went on inside, left Jason cold. *Bored* would be a better word.

He could not say the same for his copper-haired housekeeper.

A vision of Mrs. Honeywell, legs splayed open, mouth slightly parted as she cradled that hideous urn his mother insisted was valuable, flashed before him. Except in Jason's mind, she was naked. And all that glorious hair was spread around her in a ring of flame.

Jason had been married. Kept a mistress. Had discreet affairs at house parties. But not one of those women had made Jason *burn* the way Mrs. Honeywell did. He wanted to bury himself in her.

A woman who was anything but a housekeeper.

Pushing away from his ledgers, Jason duly noted that not one bit of orange fur had invaded his study the entire week. Books had not been knocked off the shelves. No expensive knickknacks broken by the sweep of a plumed tail. No sign at all of that corpulent feline known as Carrot.

Nor of Mrs. Honeywell, who often followed in the cat's wake.

Jason found himself disappointed.

Deciding to take Elizabeth to the park, he climbed up to his daughter's rooms, keeping his eyes open for a glimpse of Mrs. Honeywell. The attraction between them had been hard to miss that day outside the drawing room; the air had thickened so dramatically even his mother had noticed. Lady Trent was not pleased. She insisted Mrs. Honeywell be dismissed. Or was Jason going to emulate his father and bed the servants?

Now here she was, the object of his erotic fantasies, having a tea party with his daughter.

Jason stood just outside the door for several moments before announcing his presence, watching the pretty picture his housekeeper and daughter made. They were giggling over Carrot's apparent obsession with Miss Straw, Elizabeth's favorite doll, and pretending to be great ladies.

His heart constricted sharply as Mrs. Honeywell pressed a kiss to his daughter's cheek.

Elizabeth unfurled like the bud of a rose at the housekeeper's gentle touch.

The room smelled of musty lavender, mildew, and dust, the fault of the atrocities both Mrs. Honeywell and his daughter wore on their heads. Elizabeth's held a bowl of fruit on the brim, while his housekeeper was clad in an ostrich-feathered ensemble that could only have belonged to Jason's grandmother.

Carrot stretched and eyed Jason with feline adoration. Why the damned cat liked him, he had no idea. Mrs. Honeywell, however, seemed less pleased at his sudden appearance.

"My lord." Her luscious mouth popped open in surprise. The brim of the hat fell over one eye. A cluster of copper curls dangled above her ear.

Jason's fingers twitched as he thought of the feel of her hair between his fingers.

"Hello, my lord," Elizabeth greeted him, far too solemnly for his tastes when she'd been giggling only a moment before.

Carrot meowed. *Loudly.*

Jason raised a brow at the portly cat. "I'm the one who should be outraged. I believe you're wearing *my* cravat."

Carrot shot him a look of feline indignation, then resettled himself before a saucer of milk and what looked like some bits of chicken. His tail thumped in agitation, Carrot glaring at Jason.

Bloody cat. He crouched down to eye level with his daughter. "Hello, Elizabeth."

His daughter regarded him with profound seriousness. "Lord Montieth."

Jason wanted to hear her say Papa as she'd used to.

Small bits of sugar clung to Elizabeth's lips, probably from the biscuits she and Mrs. Honeywell had been enjoying. Her hair, a light, golden brown, hung in ringlets around her cheeks, the oversize hat nearly slipping off her head. She was incredibly precious to him, this small child. Jason never cared she hadn't been born a male; only the world did.

He held out his arms to Elizabeth, and with a small smile, she climbed into them.

Jason held her tight, feeling her small bones as her fingers clutched at his coat. Elizabeth needed a mother. A family. Not a succession of nursemaids or governesses. Women who seemed only to teach his daughter how to avoid him. And while he loved his mother, Lady Trent would be a difficult taskmaster for a young girl. His mother was too exacting by far. It would be best she remain merely Grandmama to Elizabeth.

Lifting his gaze, he saw Mrs. Honeywell, beaming with affection, all of it directed at Elizabeth. There was no guile in her lovely features. None of the charlatan Wilbert often muttered she must be, only a lingering sadness in her eyes.

The old hat tilted on her head, the feathers sprouting from the crown floating in the air as she shifted, looking away.

"Mrs. Honeywell. My apologies for interrupting your tea party. Had I known this was a formal event, I would have worn my own hat."

Elizabeth, darling thing she was, giggled into Jason's shoulder.

Mrs. Honeywell bit her lip in consternation and turned in the direction of Carrot. "We weren't expecting you, my lord." She smoothed down her skirts and sighed in resignation. "I'm sure you'll have several objections to the callers Lady Elizabeth is entertaining today, but I should like to point out, my lord, that he is not in your study."

Jason liked that she challenged him. Most women didn't. "True. I concede that point to you, Mrs. Honeywell. However, he is wearing one of my cravats."

"Are you certain?" She lifted her chin. "Perhaps I borrowed it from a footman."

The thought of her being close enough to one of his footmen sent the sharp sting of jealously through him. "I recognize my own cravat, Mrs. Honeywell."

She stretched her fingers in the direction of the thin bit of silk, meaning to remove it from Carrot's neck. "I should return the item."

The cat strenuously objected, batting her hand away with one large paw.

"*Carrot.*" She tried to grab the cat.

Carrot, ever contrary, decided to launch himself across the small table to avoid her, heading right at Jason, possibly in retaliation for having his position as the only important male in the room usurped. One paw touched down in the saucer of milk, knocking it over. Then the beast's tail landed squarely in the puddle of milk before he flicked the orange plume, spraying drops across Jason and Elizabeth.

Jason sputtered and shot Carrot a look full of murderous intent as he wiped milk from his coat, trying to keep from laughing. The cat was a menace, but Jason found he wasn't truly angry. He was too happy, with Elizabeth in his arms and Mrs. Honeywell looking beautiful in her bedraggled hat.

"Carrot." Mrs. Honeywell reached for him again. "Stop this instant."

The cat leaped onto Jason's shoulder, once more evading her outstretched fingers. Mrs. Honeywell lost her balance because she'd trapped her skirts beneath one knee.

A not uncommon occurrence for Mrs. Honeywell. He'd yet to meet anyone less graceful than his housekeeper. He found it an oddly endearing trait for such a beautiful woman.

Mrs. Honeywell's shoulder hit Jason square in the chest as she fell, which in turn toppled him over onto his back, Jason taking Elizabeth with him. Mrs. Honeywell flailed for a moment before she also landed on his chest, her eyes wide, mouth mere inches from his.

Carrot let out a loud, disgruntled meow, gave them all a pointed look, and dashed out the door, the cravat dangling from his neck.

Elizabeth wiggled out of Jason's arms. "Mr. Carrot, those are exceedingly poor manners. You've ruined the tea party and offended Lord Montieth. You shall not win the hand of Miss Straw with this sort of behavior." She continued to reprimand the large orange cat as she ran out of the room.

Sunshine and flowers.

The housekeepers from Jason's childhood had all smelled of lemon and starch—not so with Mrs. Honeywell. Of course, those housekeepers had all been matronly and mature. Not beautiful with a mass of copper-colored hair.

Soft curves molded to his chest and thighs. The brim of her hat slid across his chin as she started to lift her head, the ridiculous ostrich feathers quivering. Her hand had alighted on his chest, palm stretched over the area of his heart. She was sprawled half atop him, his thigh wedged between hers.

She wiggled.

He groaned as she brushed against a very sensitive, highly aroused part of his body.

Mrs. Honeywell's delectable mouth, with its full top lip just larger than the bottom, pursed slightly. And that copper curl, the one that often tempted him, fell from her cheek to just above his nose. She couldn't fail to notice his...attraction to her. If he moved, he'd embarrass himself further.

Eyes like bluebells under a summer sky lowered to Jason's mouth. Her breathing was soft. A small noise, one that hardened his cock to granite, came from the back of her throat.

If Jason moved his chin only an inch, their lips would touch. He could claim her mouth with his. Ravish those plump lips. He told himself to breathe. Reminded himself of all the reasons he shouldn't seduce his housekeeper. He should ignore that delicious mouth. The throbbing of his cock.

"Why is Carrot wearing one of my cravats?" he whispered against her cheek. "It isn't even tied properly."

"He was experimenting with an extravagant knot to impress you but had not the patience to twist it properly. The silk kept catching in his paws. But I think the color goes well with his fur, and Carrot was invited to tea" was her flippant response.

"I should have you sacked," he murmured, the threat sounding oddly seductive. He was so close to her he could see the darker striations of blue in her eyes. The slightest parting of her lips gave him a glimpse of her tongue, tiny and pink, edging over the bottom of her teeth.

Jason wanted that mouth, preferably on him. Anywhere. As well as her tongue. Those full lips stretched around his—

"I lost Carrot," Elizabeth announced as she skipped into the room, breaking the tension crackling in the air. Seeing them both on the floor, she plopped down next to Jason, her fingers clutching at Mrs. Honeywell's skirts. "I tried to retrieve your cravat, my lord. But Carrot was too fast."

"Fast? I find that incredibly hard to believe, Elizabeth. Carrot does nothing with expediency. He couldn't even catch a mouse the other night while you were moon bathing." His gaze slid to Mrs. Honeywell. "Are you certain we are speaking of the same cat?"

Mrs. Honeywell blinked, lowered her gaze, and attempted to untangle herself from Jason. He regretted the loss of her warmth and soft press of her breasts.

"I apologize, my lord, for my clumsiness."

"But not for the cravat?" He held on to his daughter and shifted into a sitting position. "Your lack of...*agility*, Mrs. Honeywell, gives me concern for your well-being. What's to stop you from pitching yourself into, say...an armoire?"

"How do you suppose I found these hats, my lord?"

Arousal swiftly flamed to life again inside him at her tart reply. "Or the linen closet?"

"Lost to me. Whenever I ask Wilbert, he sends me in a different direction. I believe he's deliberately attempting to cause confusion."

Jason's heart thumped about in his chest at the teasing smile trying to make its way across Mrs. Honeywell's lips. "Or headfirst into that overly decorated urn outside the drawing room."

"I don't think my head would fit, my lord."

"Carrot managed to put his entire body inside the urn, Mrs. Honeywell. That cat's backside is much larger than your head." He took in her hat. "That monstrosity notwithstanding."

"It is only Carrot's fur that makes him seem so fat." Elizabeth leaned her head against Jason's shoulder.

He looked aghast at Mrs. Honeywell. "Have you been feeding my daughter such tales? That cat weighs more than you do, Elizabeth."

Jason was rewarded with a broad smile from Mrs. Honeywell. All that sunshine and light directed at him nearly struck him dumb.

Mrs. Honeywell wobbled to her feet. She'd probably trip over her skirts on the way out. At the very least, she'd bump her knee on the door. "If you'll excuse me, my lord, I have a cat to find." Her fingers smoothed down the gray wool of her serviceable skirts.

He found her extraordinarily beautiful, even dressed like a mourning dove, with that ridiculous hat perched on her head. He wanted to dismiss her but not for Carrot or her impertinence, or even for her over familiarity with his daughter, but because then Mrs. Honeywell would no longer be in his employ. And he could pursue her without offending his honor or hers.

"Good day, my lord." She bobbed. "Lady Elizabeth." Her footsteps echoed down the hall as she went in search of Carrot, who was probably shredding Jason's cravat to bits.

"I like Ollie," Elizabeth whispered into his neck. "Do you?"

His heart actually fluttered in his chest, something he hadn't known it was capable of doing. "Yes."

CHAPTER SEVEN

S EVERAL DAYS LATER, after the tea party, Oleana found herself pacing back and forth across the tiled floors of Lord Montieth's home. She'd searched every square inch of her employer's house for any sign of orange fur. Oleana had even questioned Montieth's valet under the guise of returning the cravat, which she claimed to have found on the stairs.

Entwistle, Montieth's exacting valet, had not been fooled.

Plucking the bit of silk from her fingers, Entwistle had nearly swooned at the sight of so many tiny bite marks on his master's cravat. The silk was ruined. Destroyed. The valet had made a strange sound, probably attempting not to scream, and walked stiffly away. He had assured Oleana that should he see her *beast*, she would be informed.

None of the maids had seen Carrot. Nor the footmen. Wilbert, smug smile on his thin lips, merely crossed his arms as she went about looking for the cat.

"Ticktock," he whispered to her as she sailed by.

Oleana waited until his back was turned and stuck her tongue out at him.

She didn't need Wilbert to count down the time she had remaining as a member of Montieth's household. Oleana was eminently aware that her time here was coming to an end. She'd worried for so long that Montieth would find out her recommendation letter was written for someone else, or that Carrot would finally do something horrible, she hadn't considered being dismissed for something else entirely.

Attraction. Sheer hunger for another human being.

Oleana was no stranger to desire, having experienced some version of the emotion while wed to Percival. Nor was Oleana oblivious to her own appeal, at least before a gentleman saw her trip over a table leg or accidentally shoot a piece of roast across the room while she cut it.

Such had happened when Percival's patron, Lord Delacorte, had come to supper. Most embarrassing.

But the attraction between her and Montieth was dangerous in a way she couldn't possibly have imagined when she first assumed the position of housekeeper. He hadn't liked her for so long...and now he *did*. He'd smiled at her, or at the very least, his lips had curled into something resembling amusement. And he hadn't threatened Carrot after her cat's deplorable display of manners during the tea party.

Ah. His smile. It did strange things indeed to her insides.

A tingle shot down between her thighs, and Oleana shook her head. It was amazing she could even converse with Montieth let alone be in the same room with him. Even under the best circumstances, the fact remained that he was an earl. Oleana was far beneath him socially whether she was a housekeeper, a governess, or a vicar's widow. The most she could ever hope for was a discreet affair if Montieth were so inclined. Which he wouldn't be. Mrs. Beesom, the cook, was something of a gossip. She'd told Oleana once while kneading bread dough that there had been several housemaids over the years who had batted their eyes at Monteith, making him aware they'd welcome his attentions. He'd avoided them all. Something his father hadn't done. The previous earl had bedded anything in a skirt, whether they worked for him or not. *This* Lord Montieth, Mrs. Beesom had added, was far more honorable than his sire.

Blast.

Oleana found herself before Montieth's study, the only place she hadn't yet searched. She raised her hand to knock on the door. There were no sounds coming from within, no light beneath the door. Still, it wasn't terribly late. Possibly Montieth was already out for the evening. Carrot couldn't open doors, yet he'd vanished from her quarters.

Someone let Carrot out.

It was the only explanation that made sense.

Oleana had left Carrot on her bed this morning, sound asleep, as she'd gone down to gather Elizabeth for breakfast and a walk in the park. She had closed and locked the door behind her, put the key in her pocket.

Now he had been missing for the better part of the day.

Someone has been in my room.

Unease made her fingers unsteady as she placed her hand on the door of Montieth's study. Once Carrot was retrieved, she would seek the privacy of her room and give in to the worry hovering at the edges of her mind.

As quietly as possible, she turned the knob to enter the study, grateful the hinges had been oiled, for there was no sound as she opened the door. Carrot had an almost pathological need to lavish his affection on Monteith, the one person least likely to return it. If he was hiding anywhere, it was in the study.

Despite all the trouble Carrot caused, Oleana couldn't bring herself to give the cat away. She could have left him behind when she'd fled the Caraways but couldn't bear to. Carrot had been a gift on her twelfth birthday from her father, and Oleana's constant companion ever since. Mrs. Caraway had succeeded in taking nearly everything else away from her, but not Carrot. When Oleana's father had died suddenly, shortly after her marriage to Percival, Mrs. Caraway had immediately stepped in to sell everything before Oleana had even come out of her grief. She'd auctioned off the books Oleana's mother had so carefully collected. The furniture. The pigs her father had raised. Mrs. Caraway had declared Carrot a nuisance, insisting the vicarage could ill afford a cat who didn't earn his keep. Not to mention the orange fur Carrot left all over everything. Completely useless. Much like Oleana herself.

It was the only time Percival had stood up to his mother, declaring his new bride should keep her cat. His affection for Carrot and Oleana had faded within the year, but by that time, neither of them had had anywhere else to go.

Before she stepped inside the study, Oleana glanced up and down the hall once more to make sure Wilbert wasn't lurking about. The butler was determined to see her cast out of Montieth's home. His punishments of her varied, depending on how much sherry he'd partaken of as he sat at the head of the table in the kitchen, lording over the lesser servants. Last week, Oleana had overheard Wilbert telling George, the head groom, that if he had his way, Mrs. Honeywell would be on the first ship bound for Australia, where all criminals belonged.

Carrot was a perfect weapon in the war the butler waged against Oleana. A sure way to have her dismissed.

Wilbert was the only person in the earl's household who would have the audacity to enter Oleana's chambers and allow Carrot to escape. The butler's resentment and dislike weren't secrets among the rest of the staff. Not a day went by when there wasn't some sort of choice insult thrown in her direction. He still hadn't given Oleana the correct directions to the linen closet. One of the housemaids had slipped and admitted Wilbert had instructed the staff not to disclose the location because it amused him to send Oleana on a wild goose chase through the house.

Wilbert was such a petty human being.

Mrs. Beesom had warned her just the other day about Wilbert. The cook had been stuffing a goose when she'd caught sight of Oleana in the kitchen. Waving her over, unmindful of the bread clinging to her fingers, Mrs. Beesom had lowered her voice so only Oleana could hear. "You'd best watch out for Wilbert. He means you ill, Mrs. Honeywell."

A contented purr echoed in the study.

Carrot.

Oleana moved quietly through the darkened room, toward the sound, first banging her hip on a table near the door, then nearly running into a large, booted foot hanging off the edge of a leather sofa. Oleana covered her mouth with one hand to keep from cursing out loud.

Monteith.

Her pulse fluttered in her throat.

The room was dark, the fire giving off only a muted, flickering light. She could make out the rough outline of a large male on the sofa, but little else.

Her skin started to hum, her body instantly aware of his.

Moving toward the bookcase, Oleana squinted into the darkness, searching for Carrot. He liked to lounge about on the third row of the bookcase, somewhere between Julius Caesar and Tiberius. Terrified of waking Montieth and being caught sneaking around his study, Oleana stepped so her feet made barely a sound against the rug. Pausing, she stood still and listened, waiting for Carrot to give away his location.

A loud, seductive purr sounded. The noise came not from the bookcase but from the sofa.

Drat.

Oleana stared in quiet horror at the couch and the large male sound asleep upon it, cursing her terrible cat's ability to be in the worst places at the most inopportune times. She inched closer, against her better judgment.

The fire threw shadows over his lean form, flames glancing off the chiseled profile and broad shoulders. As he slept, the harsh lines of his handsome features were relaxed, the sensual mouth soft, the lips not tightened into any hint of a scowl. He looked younger. Less severe. The top of his shirt was unbuttoned, exposing the hollow of his throat.

Oleana stared at the small patch of skin, wanting very much to press her mouth to the spot.

A log fell into the fire, light flaring for an instant—long enough for Oleana to spy the large ball of orange fur stretched in contentment across Monteith's hips.

Carrot seemed determined to undermine Oleana's stay in Montieth's household. Regardless of their attraction for each other, she doubted Monteith's charity would extend to having Carrot sleeping on his—

Well, there were various names.

Percival had called it his manhood or spear, which had made Oleana giggle at the most unfortunate moments. There were other, more colorful names for the male appendage, most she shouldn't even know given she'd wed a vicar, but Oleana had grown up on a farm. Animals mated. The breeding of livestock required certain terms be used. And Oleana was nothing if not curious. Another sign of her lustful nature, according to her late husband.

"I should toss you into the stables myself," she whispered to the troublesome animal. "You won't get bowls of milk or wear cravats if we're thrown out into the streets." She wiggled her fingers, trying to entice Carrot to move from the lower half of Monteith's body.

A louder purr erupted. One she was sure the rest of the house could hear. Carrot's ears twitched in her direction, but he failed to move.

Oleana stepped closer, so near Montieth she caught the spicy scent of his shaving soap and pine coming from his skin as if he'd been tramping through the woods and not sitting in his study. Her only hope was in snatching Carrot up quickly and dashing out of the study and up to her room, all without waking Montieth. Leaning over, she reached for Carrot, her fingers making contact with his fur just as her wrist was circled by several large fingers.

"Oh," she sputtered, trying to back away.

The hold on her wrist tightened. Montieth's eyes flicked open. "Good evening, Mrs. Honeywell." His voice was roughened by sleep, scraping pleasurably against her. He raised his head a fraction of an inch, taking in the cat who was nesting on his…hips. A sigh of disgust left him at the sight of Carrot.

"You're awake, my lord."

"Very perceptive, Mrs. Honeywell. I also have a corpulent cat sleeping on me. Carrot has all the markings of an unwelcome suitor continuing to pay a call on a young lady who has refused him numerous times and does not wish for his attentions. In this instance, Mrs. Honeywell, I am the young lady."

Oleana had to bite her lip to keep from smiling. Montieth possessed a quick wit when he wasn't trying to intimidate others. It only added to his appeal.

"You find the situation amusing?" There was no hard edge to his words, just a teasing quality as if they were sharing a private joke.

"No, my lord. Of course not."

"How do you suppose I should I refer to him? I rather like corpulent cat. He reminds me of the older gentlemen I see at my club, so rounded their waistcoats are always in danger of bursting open if they have so much as one more plate of food."

"He does possess substantial girth, my lord." Oleana shrugged. "Oddly enough, Carrot was the runt of the litter."

Montieth shot her a curious glance.

"So I was given to understand," she hurriedly added. "From Miss Symon."

"The runt? Well, Carrot has made up for lost time, hasn't he? I suppose that's why my aunt wanted him, because he was the smallest. She'd no idea what he would grow into, did she? Naming him after a vegetable."

"His fur, I suppose, reminded Miss Symon of a carrot."

"Hmm. Still, an odd name for a cat. Speaks of a whimsical nature, which my aunt did not possess." He tugged her closer.

The combination of Montieth's comment and Oleana's own nervousness at being so close to him led her to bang her shin on the low table before the sofa, rattling the decanter of scotch. She winced but refrained from stooping to rub away the pain.

"Good Lord. How did you survive your childhood?"

"Carefully, my lord. And with a great many bruises."

A rich, decadent sound came from Montieth, startling both her and Carrot. Oleana had had no idea the sound of Monteith's laughter would brush against her body like a caress and cause such a delicious tingling down her spine.

He tugged her closer until her legs pressed into the edge of the sofa. "You must have caused your parents great concern."

"I've never been what you would call graceful."

"I don't doubt it."

"I've always tripped over my own two feet, my lord. I was once examined by a physician to ensure there was no physical reason for my inability to control my limbs." Oleana recalled that day with great clarity. Her father had been terribly concerned there was something wrong with her eyesight.

"And what was the physician's conclusion?"

"That I was merely clumsy. Nothing more. I once smacked a vicar in the cheek while trying to return a missal that had fallen to the floor in his church."

The vicar had been Percival. It was how she'd met the man who would become her husband.

Another dark chuckle left him. "You struck a man of the cloth?"

"Not intentionally. But to add to the vicar's misery, I attended the church picnic immediately following his sermon, where I managed to trip over a tree root and upend the table holding two pies and a cake." Mrs. Caraway had been furious to have her son so embarrassed, but Percival had only plucked a bit of cake from her shoulder. He'd been so lovely standing before her, licking cake off his fingers. She missed that Percival at times. But even so, Oleana had never felt for her husband what she did for the man before her. There was no comparison.

"You are dangerous, Mrs. Honeywell." Montieth's voice had lowered an octave, mixing with Carrot's low purr. "England's armies would be undefeatable should we merely allow you to lead a charge against the enemy."

His thumb gently brushed the sensitive skin of her wrist, making a circle against the soft throb of her pulse. Fire ignited from his touch, burning along the length of her arm, and spread across her chest to curl around her midsection.

"Oleana."

He'd never called her by her given name before and the sound of it on his lips, in the intimacy of the study, sent a bolt of longing through her. She should pull away. Grab Carrot and make some polite excuse before sprinting out the door. Instead, as Montieth pulled her close, she parted her lips at the expectation of finally meeting his.

Oh.

His mouth was softer than she'd imagined. There was only the barest hint of him, the taste of a much longer kiss they were meant to share. She gasped as he angled his body upward to fix his lips more firmly to hers. A growl came from him as he released her wrist, his hands moving to her waist and the back of her neck, pulling Oleana down to the lush heat promised by his mouth. He kissed Oleana as if he was starved for her, barely able to restrain himself from devouring her whole.

He isn't cold at all.

Percival had never kissed her like this. Nor had any of the village boys who'd stolen a brief peck after a dance. At the feel of his tongue against the seam of her mouth, Oleana opened her lips without hesitation, hearing the rumble of approval in his chest. She braced herself with one hand on the back of the sofa before giving up and falling forward, her hand on his hip, feeling the warm, corded muscles beneath her fingertips.

No wonder Carrot wanted to be next to Montieth. Oleana was desperate to be closer.

His hand trailed down her lower back to cup one buttock, squeezing the mound until a sound came from the back of her throat. One Oleana had never heard herself make. The tips of her breasts teased at his chest, the motion stroking her nipples into hardened peaks. She wanted to strip herself bare. Feel his skin next to hers. All her resolve to stay away from him fled in an instant under the onslaught of his mouth.

Carrot yowled, annoyed at being squished between their two bodies.

She and Montieth broke apart. Oleana's hand was very near his...*appendage*. Her other hand was nestled against his neck. His breathing was uneven. Ragged. As if he'd been running up and down the stairs. Her fingers on his hip moved, just slightly.

Montieth sucked in a breath.

They stared at each other, the only sound in the study their breathing and the fire crackling behind them. Oleana's body felt scorched. Raw.

Carrot hopped off Monteith's chest and proceeded to curl around Oleana's ankles.

Montieth's body beneath her hands grew taut. She could almost feel the chill turning him from warmth into the carved marble she so often thought him to be. He glared coldly at her, anger stamped clearly across his features.

Oleana retreated from that look, plucking her hands from his chest and straightening. "My lord—"

"Keep that animal"—the words flew at her like chips of ice—"out of my study, Mrs. Honeywell. And yourself. A momentary lack of judgment will not save you should I find Carrot in here again."

That was completely unfair.

Oleana knew she should hold her tongue and found she could not. "I grow exhausted with your threats to dismiss me because of your aunt's cat. Should you wish to do so, pray get on with it to avoid any future lapses in judgment."

"Lapses in your judgment," he snarled.

"Yes. Mine." She bent to pick up Carrot, which put her head very near Montieth's chest.

His nose grazed the top of her head. A small groan left him.

Straightening, she held the struggling Carrot against her chest. Oleana had come to London with a purpose, not only to hide but to ensure her future. Monteith had distracted her. That would stop tonight. She strode with determination toward the door. She'd saved enough to take a room in a boarding house for a month at least, if she was frugal. One that didn't mind cats. It was time she sought out Mr. Hughes.

"Good night, Mrs. Honeywell."

She paused at the door, hearing the softer tone, but did not turn around. Instead, she continued into the hall, shutting the study door behind her with a sharp click.

JASON SHOULD NOT have kissed her.

Now it would be virtually impossible to stay away from his bloody housekeeper who wasn't really a housekeeper. Nor was she a governess. Mrs. Honeywell was a temptation. A copper-haired goddess sent to upset his otherwise well-ordered life. Seducing a member of the staff was exactly the sort of thing his father had indulged in on a regular basis. The previous Lord Montieth had been a carelessly handsome rogue with a constant smile on his lips. He'd paid little attention to his wife, his son, his vast estates, or anything else but his own pleasure.

Jason desired to be nothing like him.

Yet here he was, the scent of Oleana still in his nostrils, the sweet taste of her on his lips. Carrot had finally done something for which he could be lauded, interrupting a kiss that had been rapidly escalating into something more. Perhaps, when no one else was around, Jason would scratch Carrot's ears as a reward for his very timely interruption. He'd very nearly taken Oleana on the sofa, and she wouldn't have stopped him.

Jason lay back against the leather of the couch, staring up at the ceiling, a fresh glass of scotch clasped atop his stomach, contemplating exactly what he should do about Oleana Honeywell. If he were wise, he would cease thinking of her and instead contemplate his dreadfully dull future with Miss Langham or another tedious young lady. But instead, when he thought about a mother for Elizabeth, a wife for him—

One he would take liberties with at a ball.

—all Jason could see was Oleana.

Christ. He wasn't even sure her name was truly Oleana.

The lone report Mathers had sent only told Jason there *had* been a Mrs. Honeywell employed by his aunt, but he could confirm little else save the housekeeper's first name. Aunt Agatha's former servants had scattered. Most had retired and gone to live with family. Several had died. Jason had hired the current caretaker of his aunt's estate just this year. He'd never known Aunt Agatha or her staff. His aunt had been a recluse. What few neighbors she'd possessed hadn't seen her or visited the estate in years.

"Damn," he hissed into the empty room.

Mathers had found nothing that confirmed or denied Oleana had worked for Aunt Agatha. Still, Jason found it impossible she had. She was too young, far too outspoken and lovely to have been in the employ of his cantankerous aunt.

And far too tempting to remain his housekeeper.

CHAPTER EIGHT

L EAVING LORD MONTIETH to stew in the study, her mouth still warm from his, Oleana quickly made her way to her room. Closing the door, she threw the lock before daring to set Carrot down. Then she grabbed a chair from by the window and wedged it beneath the doorknob for good measure.

Carrot yowled once more before leaping onto the bed and making himself comfortable on her pillow.

Oleana shook her head at him. "You've caused more trouble than you're worth, Carrot. Though, I must admit, tonight your timing was impeccable." Had he not objected to being pressed between her and Montieth, Oleana might well have found herself beneath Montieth on that sofa.

At least tonight's kiss had told Oleana one thing. There was nothing casual about her feelings for Montieth. Nor were those feelings purely physical. Another reason it was time for her to leave before her heart was completely lost. There was no future for her and Monteith.

Carrot rolled over onto his back and pawed at something in the air, his claws stretching and retracting.

After walking to the battered dresser against one wall, Oleana bent and opened the bottom drawer. Whoever had been in her room, and she was fairly certain it was Wilbert, hadn't disturbed anything, at least as far as she could tell. Still, Oleana would rest better if she knew her secret was still safe.

Digging through a layer of clothing in the drawer, Oleana pulled out the worn copy of *Pride and Prejudice*. It was one of only two books she'd saved from Mrs. Caraway's efforts to leave Oleana bereft of anything that belonged to her parents. She'd read the book dozens of times. Perhaps that was what accounted for her fascination with Montieth. He could very well have stepped into the role of Mr. Darcy.

Though the book was a favorite, it held no sentimental value for Oleana, but it did make an excellent hiding place. Men, Oleana had found, avoided even touching such hopelessly romantic tomes. Opening the book, she plucked out the yellowed piece of vellum thick with age and stuck firmly between two chapters.

Unfolding the fragile bit of paper, careful not to tear or crumple it between her fingers, Oleana read over the deed to her family's farm. The farm consisted of a decent amount of acreage, but the ground was poor for farming. Her father had been marginally more successful breeding pigs. When the property had come to her upon her father's death, Percival had only belabored the burden she'd put upon him. No one had been the least interested in buying her father's farm. The house had fallen into disrepair with no one to care for it.

"Worthless," Mrs. Caraway had decreed. "Much like yourself."

When Percival had died after falling from his horse, Mrs. Caraway's intention had been to send Oleana back to the farm, uncaring that the house was unlivable and Oleana lacked the funds to make repairs. She'd been one more mouth to feed, Mrs. Caraway had said, and now that they'd lost the vicarage, the Caraways could ill afford to offer Oleana charity. There was no child to keep Oleana tied to Percival's family. According to Mrs. Caraway, Oleana could take her deplorable cat and return to the farm from which she'd come.

Oh, if only it had been that easy to be free of the Caraways.

Oleana had already packed her meager possessions to return

to the farm and had come down for what she'd expected to be her last breakfast with Mrs. Caraway and Percival's stepbrother, Albert, only to find them entertaining a caller in the front parlor. The caller had been Mr. Grant Hughes from London, a gentleman who worked for the Northern Railway. He'd been making inquiries about a strip of land he'd been told belonged to the Caraways. He'd wanted to make an offer for the property, on which sat an old farm.

How foolish Oleana had been not to account for Mrs. Caraway's greed. When she'd entered the parlor that day, she'd been stupid enough to think all her problems had been solved, when in fact they'd been just beginning.

Oleana had awoken the following morning to find the door to her room locked. It would stay locked, Mrs. Caraway had informed her, until Oleana agreed to wed Albert, bringing with her the deed to the farm as her dowry. Oleana had waited for weeks, hoping someone from the village would ask to see her or notice her absence. But no one had come. After another month of seeing no one but Mrs. Caraway and the maid who'd brought her meals, Oleana had pretended to consider the offer to become Albert's wife, voicing a trembling concern that her mourning period for Percival wasn't over. And there was also the issue that Albert was Percival's brother, though not by blood.

Mrs. Caraway, thrilled that her strident methods had borne fruit, had immediately set out to visit the bishop in Shrewsbury, promising to smooth over any concerns before the banns were posted. Oleana had been permitted out of her room but watched closely by Albert on the one afternoon Mrs. Caraway had been gone.

Oleana hadn't tried to leave. Instead, she'd unlocked the liquor cabinet.

Albert liked brandy. A great deal of it. Mrs. Caraway rarely allowed him any. While he'd been busy indulging in spirits, Oleana had slipped out, Carrot in her arms, and fled. Her grandmother had lived in a village outside the grand estate where she'd once been a housekeeper. Oleana's plan had been to stay there for a while before setting out for London to find Mr. Hughes. The deed proving Oleana's ownership had been tucked firmly between the pages of her favorite book. Mrs. Caraway knew nothing of Oleana's family. She wouldn't know to look for her in a tiny village with the name of Badger.

Sadly, Grandmother had died shortly after Oleana's arrival.

Oleana carefully refolded the paper, placing it back between the pages of *Pride and Prejudice*. After sliding the book beneath a pile of her underthings until it was hidden, she shut the drawer.

The letter of recommendation from Miss Symon for her former housekeeper had been pressed into Oleana's hand as her grandmother had lain dying. She'd been far too old and infirm to travel to London and assume the responsibilities of housekeeper for an earl. Nor had she wanted to leave Badger. Oleana had protested, but her grandmother had insisted, saying that Mrs. Caraway would eventually come there, and when she did, Oleana best be gone. Oleana had to go to London, secure a position with the Earl of Montieth to hide herself from the Caraways, and find Mr. Hughes.

So she had. Or at least, she'd accomplished some of what she'd set out to do.

After readying herself for bed, Oleana lay beside a purring Carrot, her worried mind anxiously toying with her future. She held the deed to the farm. Surely it couldn't be too difficult to find Mr. Hughes or the offices of the Northern Railway. She would present the deed as proof of her ownership and sell to him immediately. Hire a solicitor. Move somewhere as far from Mrs. Caraway and Albert as she could.

The risk was in revealing herself to Mr. Hughes. He could well be in league with Mrs. Caraway. But she had little choice.

After tossing and turning for the better part of an hour, Oleana decided a cup of chamomile tea might help her find some peace. The house was quiet, the other servants having retired long ago. It was unlikely Wilbert would be hovering about in the hall, prepared to interrogate her over some petty matter. Taking up the lamp, Oleana headed to the kitchen.

CHAPTER NINE

A FLOORBOARD CREAKED somewhere in the house. A muffled oath sounded as if someone had hurt themselves, perhaps stubbed a toe. The banister did jut out at an odd angle, and in the dark, it was easy enough to bang a limb against the wood. An architectural mistake Jason's grandfather, who'd had the London house built, had never seen fit to correct.

Could it be one of the maids? Or a footman?

Jason suspected it was neither.

After placing his now empty glass on the table, he made his way to the study door, opening it out into the muted light of the hallway. He stayed still, listening for any sound in the silent house.

The light of a lamp bobbed in the near blackness, throwing shadows against the walls. He caught a flash of white disappearing around a corner. Copper gleamed briefly where the light touched her hair before disappearing once more.

Oleana.

Jason watched as the lamp she held moved in the direction of the kitchen, debating the wisdom of pursuing her. On one hand, the thought of Oleana barely clothed and wandering about at night was making his cock hard, a sure sign he should return to the study, or better yet, seek out his own bed. But on the other hand, it was the middle of the night. What was she doing wandering about?

Perhaps he should just make sure she wasn't trying to steal the silver. Or murder Wilbert in his bed.

He crept silently behind her, watching as her slight form entered the kitchen and she set the lamp on the large worktable. She bustled about, nightgown flowing around her ankles, kettle in hand as she set about making tea.

Yes, incredibly nefarious, the making of tea.

Reaching up to a shelf, she grabbed the tin where he assumed the tea was kept.

He tried not to focus on the way the nightgown snaked up her body as she stretched her fingers across the top of the shelf. A soft melody came to him in the darkness. Oleana was humming, though Jason couldn't make out the tune. He took one step back up the stairs, meaning to leave and seek his bed. This was madness. Torture.

Oleana moved to stand before the fire.

Jesus.

The contour of her body was clearly visible through the thin wisp of cotton pretending to be a nightgown. When she turned, he devoured the sight of her full, round breasts, with the tiny peaks of her nipples outlined against the light.

Jason shut his eyes, arousal winding itself around his entire lower body. *Madness.* This was madness.

"Damn and blast," she uttered as she turned, banging her shin on what he assumed was the leg of the worktable.

Jason had never in his entire life known a woman to bump into so many things on a regular basis. She'd nearly elbowed him in the nose when he'd kissed her earlier.

His eyes snapped open again to find her bending over to rub her much abused shin, giving him a lovely view of her backside. He curled his fingers, remembering the feel of all that softness cupped in his palms earlier. Coming further down the stairs, he knew the moment she heard his footsteps.

"My lord." Oleana straightened, looking over her shoulder at him. "Good evening."

"Mrs. Honeywell." His voice sounded incredibly loud in the confines of the kitchen.

She gestured to the tin, seemingly unconcerned to be found in a state of undress before him. "I'm having trouble sleeping and thought a cup of tea might help. Would you care for one?"

"No, thank you." Jason took a deep breath and walked further into the kitchen, gaze sweeping over her body clad in the nightgown down to her bare toes peeking out from beneath the hem.

Insanity. Pure insanity.

Assured they were alone, he moved in her direction, drawn by some unseen force to Oleana, though his mind screamed for his retreat. There was only an arm's length and a bit of cotton separating him from the curves of her body.

"I forgot my slippers," she said, attempting to hide her bare feet beneath the hem of her nightgown.

"I don't believe a pair of slippers would have kept you from stubbing your toes any number of times. I heard you cursing as you made your way down here." He held up three fingers. "Three times, if one is counting, which I was. Are you certain it isn't your eyesight?"

"I see perfectly well," she replied. "But there are unforeseen obstacles in this house, my lord. Part of the banister sticks out at an odd angle. Hallways filled with useless ferns that I suppose one should consider decorative."

"My mother's doing," he stated. "Not the banister but the ferns."

"Well, it is unsettling to walk down the hall with only a lamp and then feel the brush of those fronds against one's skin. Like the touch of a ghost."

"And do you believe in ghosts, Mrs. Honeywell?" He wasn't sure how they'd come to discussing ferns and ghosts, but Jason found the way her mind jumped about fascinating.

"Sometimes." She cocked her head. "I believe we are all haunted by something."

He thought Oleana might be. Perhaps that was what had brought her to London. "I would have to agree. Is that what kept you awake tonight? Your own personal haunting?"

Oleana's features grew shadowed as he took another step. If he leaned in, the tips of her breasts would brush against his chest. The light floral scent that seemed to hover about her invaded Jason's nostrils, making him dizzy with lust.

"Our earlier encounter—" he started.

Oleana arched just slightly in his direction at the mention of their kiss, her gaze landing on his mouth for the briefest moment.

"—led me to thoughts of Aunt Agatha. I was trying to recall the village just outside her estate. The name escapes me."

"Badger, my lord. Not the least notable, though the pub there does make a very fine rabbit stew, and they hold a splendid fair in the spring."

The bit about the pub was certainly true. He'd eaten there years ago. Jason wasn't sure about the fair, but her words held a ring of truth—enough to keep him from accusing her outright of lying to him. "How did you come to work for my aunt again? I find it odd we never crossed paths."

"Not so unusual, my lord. Your visits were short and not frequent." A lucky guess on her part. "Are you questioning my letter of recommendation? It was written in Miss Symon's own hand." Her gaze fluttered to his mouth once again.

"Yes, the letter spoke of years of service." Jason wasn't sure what this middle-of-the-night interrogation was meant to do other than arouse him further. At the moment, his desire for her outweighed any of his suspicions and every honorable thought he'd once had of leaving this kitchen without touching her. "A glowing recommendation of your talents." He leaned in toward her neck, inhaling the scented warmth of her skin.

"My lord, forgive me," she breathed. "But it is the middle of the night. Could we continue this discussion of my qualifications tomorrow?"

"I'd prefer to have it now." Dear God, he wanted to taste her again.

"I started in the scullery, in your aunt's kitchen." She turned away, giving him the line of her neck. "Worked my way up to assisting the cook."

"Mrs. Fordam. Lovely woman. Makes a splendid gooseberry pie. Don't you agree?"

Oleana nodded. "I adore a good gooseberry pie, and Mrs. Fordam's was one of the best."

Mrs. Fordam had been a woman nearly as elderly as Aunt Agatha. She'd made terrible pies. "You and my aunt must have been very close."

She wasn't looking in his direction but toward the fire. "In a manner of speaking, my lord. We only knew each other a short time but got on well."

"And yet after such a brief acquaintance, she left you her most treasured possession."

Oleana turned back to him, her brow wrinkled just slightly.

"Carrot is what I refer to, Mrs. Honeywell. She did bequeath the care of her cat to you."

"Yes. Of course. I don't think of him as a possession, my lord. Carrot is almost a person." The kettle began to whistle, and she slipped by him, picking up a rag from the table. "At least he feels he is. Blast." Whipping around, she held the kettle in one hand, a finger in her mouth.

Christ. He'd never thought a woman burning her finger could be so erotic.

"You may add this to my list of clumsy attributes, my lord. I burned myself." She held up her finger. "Although, in my defense, I was distracted." She moved before the firelight once more and set down the kettle. Either Oleana was completely unaware of the transparency of her nightgown or she was deliberately trying to torture him.

Sheer madness.

"You may need to keep your distance from the fire," Jason choked out. "If you wish to hold on to your modesty, Mrs.

Honeywell."

She turned so abruptly at his words the hem of her night-gown caught in her toe. Or her heel. It didn't matter. As she teetered forward, her head fell toward the corner of the table, and Jason reached out, grabbing her firmly about the waist before she could harm herself.

He held on to her, keeping one arm draped around her middle. "You are a walking disaster."

"So I've been told."

He wanted to eat her whole. Strip the wisp of cotton from her body and nibble against her skin. Instead, he brushed his lips along the graceful line of her neck, touching the flesh with his tongue. The thick copper of her hair was wound into a braid, and Jason picked up the heavy weight, wrapping the braid around his wrist before pulling her mouth to his.

"You can't possibly be who you pretend," he murmured against her lips.

"Then why not dismiss me outright? If you are so certain."

Because he *couldn't*. Didn't want to. Especially with those lovely breasts teasing against his chest. He tightened his hold on the braid, pulling back her head until the column of her throat lay bared in invitation before him.

"I should." Jason's nose trailed along the slope of her shoulder, wildflowers and sunshine. He flicked out his tongue against the lobe of her ear before nibbling gently.

A soft moan came from her. "I could leave in the morning, if you like."

Jason lifted her, sighing at the way his fingers sank into the curves of her flesh. He nudged her legs apart to stand between them, breathing her in, his hands sliding up the bow of her waist.

Such wonderful madness. Jason wished never to feel sane again.

"No." He pressed a kiss to the corner of her mouth, hearing her intake of breath. She was tugging at his shirt, her fingers tracing his muscles. "I—don't want to let you go. Honestly, I don't think I can, Oleana."

Another soft sound came from her at his words. Jason cupped one breast, stroking her through the fabric. He sought the taut peak of her nipple, rolling the tip gently between his fingers. He lowered his mouth to suckle her through the thin cotton.

She arched more fully against him, begging him with her body for more. There was no hesitation in her actions. No apprehension or reticence.

"I know my own mind," Oleana said in a quiet voice. Her fingers threaded through his hair, tugging at the strands. "I have no expectations of you beyond tonight."

"Maybe you should." Jason pushed her down to lie on the table, shoving her nightgown up further. He could smell her arousal for him, filling the air of the kitchen. He trailed his fingers down the inside of one thigh, marveling at the feel of her skin. Like silk. He sank a finger inside her, and she gasped at the sensation, then opened herself further to him, her hips pushing up against his hand. While stroking gently with his thumb at the flesh hidden between her folds, Jason tugged at the opening of her nightgown, sending the buttons popping, baring one gorgeously rounded breast. He teased the nipple with his nose before sucking the delicate tip into his mouth.

Another finger joined the first, Jason pressing down lightly with his thumb on the sensitive bit of flesh before retreating. He lifted his head to see her beautiful face flush, glowing softly in the muted light of the fire. Oleana twisted sensuously on the table.

She was the most beautiful thing he'd ever seen.

A whimper came from her, the muscles surrounding his fingers tightening as she chased her release. Her body tensed, eyes opening as she climaxed, a soft feminine sound of absolute bliss escaping her parted lips. Oleana lay panting softly as his hands left her. When he tried to step back, Oleana reached out, her fingers taking hold of his wrist.

"More," she whispered.

"Yes." Jason heard his own voice, rough with desire. He kissed his way slowly up her stomach, pushing up her nightgown further. His palm fell possessively over her ribs. "I want you. But I will stop should you not wish—"

"I wish." Oleana clutched his shoulders, the strands of his hair, pulling and tugging at him with an appetite that matched his own. She tore at his trousers, pausing only to wrap her fingers around the length of his cock before lying back and offering herself to him.

Their joining was ferocious. Fierce. Awkward somewhat, as it was accomplished across the same wooden table that had been used only hours ago to prepare dinner. Jason took her hard, his hunger for her such that he couldn't be gentle. She matched every thrust, wrapping her legs around his hips, her heels digging into the backs of his thighs. They were savages, grasping and tearing at each other with such violence it took Jason's breath away. When Oleana's back bowed against the table, every muscle in her body tightening, Jason's mouth fell on hers, stifling her scream of pleasure. And his own.

He wanted this moment to last forever, because it could never happen again.

CHAPTER TEN

O LEANA TRIED MIGHTILY to regain what little senses she had left as she struggled to take a full breath. Her heart was racing in her chest, pounding so hard it nearly blotted out everything else. The wood of the worktable dug into her backside as the last remnants of the pleasure she'd just experienced pulsed through her body.

My goodness.

She had never thought to experience such…passion in her life. The marital bed with Percival had been mildly satisfying. His attentions had left her content until she'd begun to ask him for more. But never had she thought the joining of a man and woman could be so raw. Savagely intimate. As if Montieth meant to take Oleana's soul from her body with every hard thrust inside her.

She stroked the side of his face, the brush of hair along his jaw chafing her palm, enjoying the feel of his weight atop her. Oleana felt safe here within the circle of his arms. Protected.

"Montieth." She considered telling him everything. The Caraways. Mr. Hughes. All of it.

The muscles of his big body tensed an instant before he gently pulled away from her, his gaze averted as he refused to look in her direction. He started to adjust his clothing, the movements jerky. Angry.

She reached out her hand, frowning as he stepped away,

regretting the chill she could already see forming across his handsome features.

"This should not have happened." His lovely mouth, the lips that had kissed her with no hint of coldness, only passion, tilted into a scowl. "And won't happen again."

The words hissed through the quiet of the kitchen, almost accusatory in nature, filling her with a most unwelcome feeling. She'd experienced such joy with Montieth only moments ago. "You are not your father," she said quietly, remembering the stories Mrs. Beesom had told her.

"How would you know anything about my father?" he snarled back at her. "You're a bloody housekeeper and not a very good one."

Oleana fell back as if he'd slapped her. He was angry. Blamed Oleana for what had happened between them, which was completely unfair. "Agreed," she shot back.

Steeling herself, she hopped off the table and smoothed down her nightgown. Gliding over to the teapot, she turned her back to him and poured the still-hot water over the tea, though she no longer wanted a cup. Oleana wanted nothing more than a moment to collect her thoughts without him watching her. "Good night, my lord."

Montieth made a sound behind her. A growl, perhaps of annoyance.

Really, what was it he wanted her to say or do?

Oleana continued to steep the tea, pretending nothing at all was amiss, as if he hadn't just taken her like some Viking raider on a worktable in the kitchen. Yes, she was amusing. Had lovely ankles. Was delightfully clumsy. But in the end, she was only a vicar's widow pretending to be a skilled housekeeper, and not doing very well at that if Montieth's suspicions were any indication. Oleana didn't expect a sudden declaration of love or a proposal of marriage after what had occurred. But she did think she deserved to not be treated as if she was a—

"Is there something else you require, my lord?"

"No. Nothing else, Mrs. Honeywell." His voice was chilled. Like tiny bits of ice. He spun on his heel and stomped away from her, leaving the kitchen without once looking back at her.

When the sound of his heavy tread on the stairs finally faded, Oleana sagged against the worktable, wiping angrily at the tears sliding down her cheeks. She sipped her lukewarm tea and wished with all her heart she'd never made the acquaintance of the Earl of Montieth.

CHAPTER ELEVEN

"I WAS CONCERNED for a time that you wouldn't come to your senses regarding Miss Langham, Montieth. But never fear, I've an entire list of young ladies who would suit, if you suddenly decide again she will not," Lady Trent said.

"She's fine." Jason couldn't care less whom he wed. He should have known that was his mother's purpose in arriving on his doorstep today: Miss Langham. Unfortunately, he had no thoughts on the girl his mother wished him to marry. All Jason could think of was Oleana. He'd taken her like some ravenous animal in the kitchen. Any of the servants could have walked in and seen them. Disgusted with himself, he'd vowed to never touch her again.

Oleana, seeming to guess at his mood, gave him a wide berth lately, avoiding him at every turn. Jason knew he should dismiss her, but he couldn't bear the thought of her absence. For not only Elizabeth's sake but his own.

He pressed a hand over the ache in his chest.

Jason only caught fleeting glances of Oleana as she moved about his house. Sometimes he would see her copper-colored head bent to Elizabeth's as they chattered like two old matrons in the garden, pulling weeds and discussing herbs. If he passed Elizabeth's playroom at just the right time, giggles would meet his ears, along with the clink of cups as they held another tea party. He was never invited to attend.

Even the bloody cat avoided him.

"Fine?" his mother intoned, her frustration with him clear. "I'd hoped you'd find Miss Langham more than *fine*. She'll make an excellent wife and a wonderful mother for Elizabeth. Much better than having my granddaughter keeping company with your housekeeper, who I'm certain isn't well trained at anything. Do you know that when I arrived today, Elizabeth thrust a sprig of rosemary at me?"

"The utter horror." Jason tapped his forefinger against his lips. "I'm surprised you didn't swoon."

"My point"—his mother rounded on him—"is that she should be learning her sums and letters. Not the best way to grow a parsnip."

Jason mulled over that for a moment, thinking of the careful stacks of weeds and the way Elizabeth counted them. "Elizabeth is far happier with Mrs. Honeywell than any of the previous, heavily recommended women who came before. She's learning her sums. And I'm certain she's been taught to spell rosemary. Did you know Miss Abercrombie insisted to me that Elizabeth wasn't intelligent? Is that what you want for your granddaughter?"

"Of course not. I only want her to have a proper education. And how dare that woman insinuate Elizabeth isn't brilliant." His mother paced back and forth across the room several times before halting once again before him. "But even so, you aren't fooling me. Mrs. Honeywell is completely inept. And while I'm happy to hear she is good company for Elizabeth, she was hired to be a housekeeper, though Wilbert doesn't believe she was ever employed by your aunt. Her letter of recommendation was likely forged."

"I saw Aunt Agatha's signature myself. It is her handwriting."

"Then perhaps the letter was written under duress. Wilbert thinks she's a criminal—"

"Mother, do you truly believe Aunt Agatha could be coerced into doing anything she doesn't want? If Mrs. Honeywell were a criminal, wouldn't it have made more sense for her to coerce my aunt into altering her will, perhaps, instead of a letter of recommendation to be a housekeeper?"

His mother sniffed and resumed her pacing.

"Wilbert often exaggerates. His dislike of Mrs. Honeywell has led him to make baseless accusations," Jason said smoothly.

"And your attraction to her causes you to overlook her deficits."

"Is there a point to this conversation, Mother?" Jason snapped.

"Only that your father was also tempted by such things." Her voice shook. "You aren't keeping her employed for Elizabeth's sake. She's pretty, I suppose, if you don't mind the loud color of her hair."

Jason *adored* the color of Oleana's hair.

"Is that why your enthusiasm has dimmed for Miss Langham? Because of your housekeeper? *Really*, Jason."

His mother only ever called him by his Christian name when she was attempting to make a point. Or when she was distraught. Today it was probably both. Jason's father hadn't been an unkind man, but he had been careless in his treatment of his wife. Their marriage hadn't been a love match. The previous Lord Monteith's indiscretions with women of his own class had been unwelcome but tolerated. His wanderings among the female servants, however, had humiliated his mother.

"She's beneath you. If you must make her your mistress—" She waved a gloved hand. "Well, I suppose you must. Find her a lovely house you can visit when the mood strikes. But do not dawdle with the help while your daughter is under the same roof. The servants will talk. Gossip will start."

"I'm not dawdling with the help, Mother," he said, struggling to keep the vision of Oleana spread beneath him in the kitchen from his head.

"Good."

"You've yet to declare a reason for your visit." At least he'd sworn not to dawdle with Oleana again. "Is there something other than your determination to see me wed?"

"I thought, since you'll be busy spending your time courting Miss Langham—"

Jason raised a brow.

"—or another young lady equally suitable, that perhaps I should take Elizabeth with me to Eldridge Court."

"Leaving town so soon?" Eldridge Court was the country estate of his mother's husband, Lord Trent.

Mother gave a graceful wave of one gloved hand. "Lord Trent doesn't like to be away from his horses too long." His mother gave a small frown. "So we are leaving for the country at the end of the week. I thought it would be a good time to take Elizabeth for a brief respite."

What his mother really meant to do, under the guise of taking Elizabeth to her country estate, was keep his daughter from the influence of Mrs. Honeywell.

"Elizabeth adores the country," Lady Trent said. "She'll have a marvelous time."

She would. Elizabeth loved trailing behind Lord Trent as he wandered about the stables, inspecting his horses. Until Mathers returned with his full report and Jason got his...urges under control, it *would* be best for his daughter not to be in London. Especially if he had to ask Oleana to leave.

The mere thought of her not being under his roof caused another crease of pain along his chest.

"I think it's a wonderful idea, Mother." He waved Lady Trent out of the drawing room. "Let us find Elizabeth and let her know."

CHAPTER TWELVE

OLEANA WALKED ALONG the winding path in the park, listening to the sound of the gravel beneath her feet as she stared across the Serpentine. The day was cloudy with only a slight chill. A brilliant day for walking about and mulling over your future. She had little else to do. Now that Elizabeth had gone to the country with Lady Trent, Oleana's prime responsibility had disappeared. Montieth's household certainly didn't require her meager talents. She'd already weeded the small kitchen garden, something she did more for her own amusement than anything. No, there was absolutely nothing to deter Oleana from her mission of taking a long, leisurely walk in the park. Not even Wilbert sneering at her as she donned her cloak.

Montieth might have deterred her. Possibly. Had he the least interest in her. Which he did not.

She remembered every sound between them that night in the kitchen. The way his body had thrust into hers as he'd taken her. The memory caused a slow, warm twist of honey between her thighs, as it did whenever she relived the passion of their joining, something Oleana did regularly as she went about her nonexistent duties. Montieth hadn't once looked in her direction since that night, nor spoken to her.

It's for the best.

Losing one's heart to one's employer while engaged in a tawdry affair with him wasn't wise.

Her nose wrinkled. *Not* a tawdry affair. More indiscretion. Still unwise.

A breeze tugged at the strands of her hair, the ribbons of her bonnet fluttering wildly against her chin. Just as she suspected even before their…indiscretion in the kitchen, Oleana could not stay in the employ of Lord Montieth. Wilbert's dislike of her had reached new heights. Montieth was already suspicious of the half truths she'd told him. And she risked hurting Elizabeth by allowing their temporary attachment to continue.

Then there was the matter of her own heart. Already compromised.

It was well past time she sought Mr. Hughes.

Oleana's neck prickled in an unsettling manner as she looked out over the water. She turned in a half circle. The same feeling had come to her when she and Elizabeth had visited the park several days ago. As if someone was watching. But Oleana saw no one paying her the slightest mind.

She blamed her apprehension over the Caraways and her decision to go to Mr. Hughes.

Children laughed in the distance as she turned to head back in the direction from which she'd come, thinking about her attempt to reach Mr. Hughes. Oleana had made discreet inquiries from one of the footmen as to the location of the offices of the Northern Railway. He'd even offered to escort her, though Oleana had declined. James would have made her feel safer, but he might also have informed Wilbert. Which would raise more questions that Oleana didn't want to answer.

Instead, she'd taken a hack to the Northern Railway offices and, chin held high, marched inside and asked for Mr. Hughes. A clerk at the desk had greeted her politely but informed Oleana that Mr. Hughes was not in London at present but expected to return in a day or so. Frustrated after having come so far, Oleana had scratched out a message to Mr. Hughes reminding him of their brief acquaintance and leaving the address where she could be reached. He'd struck her as an honest gentleman when he'd called upon Mrs. Caraway. She was hopeful her observation wasn't wrong. After thanking the clerk, Oleana had hurried away, looking over her shoulder the entire time.

She slowed on the path, stopping before a small rise. The water was so lovely with the sun shining upon the surface. A small group of tiny boats bobbed along in the waves, a herd of children pursuing the boats, yelling and pointing at them. A governess, followed closely by a maid, trailed the children, shouting instructions and admonishing one boy, who'd gotten too close to the water. When the children and governesses finally passed, Oleana's neck tingled once more, and she turned to face a small grouping of trees.

A man lounged against the trunk of an enormous oak tree, his hat pulled low over his forehead, obscuring his features. A paper was open in one hand, giving anyone observing him the idea he was merely enjoying the park and engrossed in his newspaper.

But Oleana had the impression that what he was really doing was looking at *her*.

Panic seeped into her bones, though it was perfectly normal for a gentleman to admire a lady while relaxing in the park. The urge to run all the way to the safety of Lord Montieth's had her turning, but she maintained her pace and made for the exit. Oleana took a deep breath, reminding herself she was in full view of at least a dozen people, none of whom would allow her to be abducted in broad daylight.

At least, she hoped they wouldn't.

I'm being ridiculous.

It took what felt like years to reach the edge of the park, but when the street came into view, Oleana dared a look over her shoulder. No one followed her. Still, her heart refused to stop racing. Taking a large swallow of air, Oleana smoothed down her skirts and strolled in the direction of Lord Montieth's home, peeking behind her every so often.

I'm making much out of nothing.

Even so, she traveled the long way back to Monteith's, taking the time to hide behind a large evergreen and examine the street in both directions. Feeling foolish after several odd looks thrown in her direction, Oleana shook her head and hurried the rest of the way home.

CHAPTER THIRTEEN

J ASON DIDN'T WANT to be at a ball this evening. The crush at the home of Lord Danvers had been annoying but tolerable. This event, however, paled in comparison. His mother must have told every eligible young lady in London that her son was looking for a suitable bride. At least three women had dropped their fans in front of him in the space of an hour. Lashes were batted so often in his direction he thought every woman at the ball besieged by a fit of apoplexy. He was so bored he was afraid he'd doze off from his place at the wall.

Another promise to his mother he shouldn't have made: to attend this dull affair that was Lady Alexander's fete. Along with the vow to receive Lady Langham and her daughter when they came to call, which thankfully they hadn't. Yet.

"God, you've turned into an awful bore, Montieth." The Earl of Huntly looked down on Jason from his greater height, dressed in perfectly fitted evening clothes. Jason was tall, but Huntly was built like a small mountain. The elegant formal wear he had donned did little to stop the comparison.

"I've always been a bore, Hunt. Surely you've noticed before now."

"We've all taken note, Montieth. Do you do anything with your time other than being honorable with a scowl on your lips?" Huntly's massive shoulders shifted as if he was marching. "Tromping about being very regal and earl-like. Doesn't it become tedious? Lord knows we're all exhausted from watching."

Montieth shot him a bland look. "Says the man who until recently was regarded as the most disliked title in all of London. Now look at you, Hunt. Dressed finer than any dandy. Managing not to drop things in the punch bowl or trod on the skirts of young ladies."

Huntly grinned, not the least insulted. "True. True. Though, it was only the skirt of that one girl during Lady Trent's ball that put me in such poor standing with her. And a buffet was being served, as I recall. I'm sure I'm not the only one who may have let something slip into the punch. Probably helped the taste."

"Marriage agrees with you, Hunt." His friend glowed with happiness, a state Jason wouldn't have thought Huntly capable. Jason caught sight of the reason for Huntly's dramatic change, his wife, Emmagene, standing across the room. She was pretending to be interested in the conversation of a group of ladies around her, hiding her own boredom behind an extravagantly painted fan she snapped every so often in annoyance.

"Emmagene looks lovely, by the way. I meant to tell you so when I caught you groping each other on the terrace at Danvers's ball."

"Wasn't groping." Hunt's eyes were on the slender woman across the room. "Well"—he shrugged—"it isn't considered groping when the woman in question is your wife. Especially when she squeezes back."

"Still." Jason gave him a sideways glance. "I'm thrilled she doesn't look as if she's about to attend a funeral." Emmagene had been infamous in the past for dressing in horrible dark colors that nearly resembled widow's weeds. Not so tonight.

"A condition of our marriage." Huntly let out a booming laugh, his eyes softening as his gaze landed on his wife. "She must wear colors. No hint of black or brown. And little else beneath." Huntly wiggled his brows. "Oh, don't scowl, Montieth. You'll drive the fair Miss Langham away if she sees."

Jason took in the young woman circling the ballroom, obviously searching for him. He'd deserted her after their dance, not wanting to endure any more of her twittering conversation. Jason slid behind Huntly. He'd had quite enough of Miss Langham this evening.

"Coward," Huntly said, pulling a flask from his coat pocket. "Your behavior tells me you aren't as happy with Lady Trent's plans for your future as she is."

Jason shrugged. The thought of wedding Miss Langham left him cold. He imagined listening to her chattering for hours. Perhaps he could learn to sleep with his eyes open. Bedding her would present a struggle.

"What's wrong with Miss Langham?"

"Nothing, I suppose." *Except she's much too graceful and doesn't have hair the color of a sunset.* Jason took the offered flask, swallowing several mouths of scotch. The warmth burned into his stomach and down his legs. "She's suitable, I suppose."

"A resounding endorsement for Miss Langham." Huntly peered down at him. "Who is she?"

Jason sighed, collecting the facts. "The daughter of Lord—"

"No, you bloody scowling ogre. I know who Jane Langham's father is. I meant the woman you obviously *prefer* to Miss Langham. Is she not suitable enough to wed the illustrious Lord Montieth?"

Jason took the flask from him again. "She isn't here. She doesn't attend...these types of events."

Hunt's look grew curious before his eyes widened. "Oh. I see."

Jason paused with the flask at his lips. "You don't."

Huntly couldn't possibly. Earls didn't marry their housekeepers. They didn't even marry their false housekeepers. An additional image of Oleana panting with pleasure beneath him had Jason taking another large swallow of the scotch.

"You know, Montieth," Huntly said in a matter-of-fact tone, "there were some who decried my marriage to Emmie. Me, the most obnoxious gentleman in London, marrying an avowed spinster was looked down upon by some because the Stitch family isn't as highborn as my own. It was rather off-putting considering no one else found me to be a suitable husband. I'm fortunate Emmie agreed to wed me, earl or not."

"I concur." Montieth allowed a small smile to pull at his lips. "You are a most lucky man." Lady Huntly was waspish, difficult, and incredibly outspoken. But she was devoted to Huntly.

Almost as if she sensed her name being mentioned, Lady Huntly tossed a pleading look in her husband's direction.

Huntly waved at her. "My wife is hoping for a rescue, but if I am made to attend these events, she must suffer it as well." He turned his attention back to Jason. "I will assume this woman who has caught your eye doesn't have a lineage stretching back a century. But yours does, Montieth. You can do whatever you wish, really. Your mother might make such a choice difficult, but Lady Trent would eventually come around."

Jason sagged against the wall. "Far worse than that." He stopped short of informing Hunt the woman he craved was his housekeeper. Likely hired with a letter of false recommendation because Jason couldn't see past the gorgeous copper of her hair.

"Can you make her your mistress?" Hunt asked quietly. "Would she be open to it?"

Jason kept his eyes on the crowd before him. "I don't—" The very idea felt wrong to him, though it was a feasible solution. "No. I don't think she would be open to such an arrangement." Yes, he'd once considered making Oleana his mistress, flirted with the idea. But now knowing her, seeing her love for his daughter, having experienced her warmth and passionate nature, he couldn't—

"I see," Hunt said again, this time with more sympathy. "There are other women, Montieth. Ones with more palatable backgrounds, perhaps. Though, if it were me, I wouldn't let honor or duty stand in the way of happiness."

Jason whirled back to his friend, suddenly so incredibly angry he thought he might explode. "You've no idea, Hunt. *You* who have never done anything honorable in your entire fucking life. It isn't a question of what I want."

"Well, maybe it should be. Miss Langham reminds me a great deal of your late wife. I never thought I'd see you wed another porcelain doll more appropriate for setting on the mantel in your drawing room than bedding."

"Good evening," Jason snarled, close to punching Huntly in the face. He made his way out of the ballroom, sailing past Miss Langham without a word.

He was so bloody angry.

Because Huntly was right.

CHAPTER FOURTEEN

OLEANA TOSSED AND turned, unable to fall back asleep after a horrible nightmare in which she'd dreamed Percival was still alive and he'd found her in bed with Montieth. Percival had been screaming she was a liar, a harlot, and a vicar's wife.

Had it been a mistake to seek out Mr. Hughes? The Caraways might be having his offices watched. She'd been so distraught today after her walk in the park that she'd finally made her way to the linen closet. The rest of the afternoon was spent counting out the number of sheets and tablecloths. Afterward, Oleana had pretended to check the contents of the larder under the amused eye of Mrs. Beesom, who'd found the proceedings vastly amusing. Next, Oleana had checked with the upstairs maid to ensure there was a sufficient supply of beeswax.

Everything was, of course, well in order. Wilbert might be a tyrant, but he was an efficient one.

It wasn't the first time she'd realized how unnecessary she was since coming to Montieth's home, but usually Oleana consoled herself with the fact that she was making a difference in Elizabeth's life.

Wilbert had followed Oleana about, eyeing her with smug dislike, nostrils flaring as she passed. "I do hope your things are packed," he'd said. "I doubt you'll be staying much longer."

"Ugh." She slammed her palms down on the bed, startling Carrot.

The big cat opened one eye and gave her a scathing look before rolling over.

"Sorry." Oleana ran her fingers through Carrot's fur. She wasn't in the mood for tea, but perhaps a good book, one not hiding the deed to her father's farm, might be useful in helping her sleep. Montieth did possess a library, a rather fine one. She often sat inside with Elizabeth on rainy days, reading to her young charge while the fire crackled away. The library was bound to have a great number of tedious volumes on farming techniques or military history. Oleana didn't hold out much hope for a gothic novel or anything the least feminine in nature.

She'd heard the carriage brought around earlier and knew that Montieth had gone out for the evening. Mrs. Beesom had said earlier that His Lordship was dining at his club before attending some ball. Or maybe the theater.

Oleana shook her head at the hollowness filling her chest, thinking of Montieth spinning about some faceless young lady. It didn't matter, she told herself. What was important was Monteith wasn't at home. She remembered quite well what had occurred the last time she'd gone sneaking about the house.

Warmth lapped down between her thighs, and her breasts tingled at the memory.

"Oh, good Lord." Jumping up from the bed, Oleana smoothed down the gray wool of her skirts. Thankfully, she was still dressed. Taking up a lamp, she made her way quietly down the stairs to the library.

The scent of books and leather filled her nostrils as she wandered into the room, lamp held high so she could clearly see the path before her. Tripping over a table or breaking something would only draw Wilbert's attention, and she was in no mood to be reprimanded. No fire had been lit, and the air was chilly, but Oleana didn't expect to be long. Holding the lamp higher, she ran the light over the bookcase before her.

"Dull," she whispered to an entire section on the architecture of medieval castles. "Dreadfully dull." She rolled her eyes at seeing another section on Sparta. "Horrifyingly tedious." This entire row was on the trade routes of the Phoenicians. Moving further to the right, Oleana finally found what she was looking for, tucked on the lowest shelf. An entire collection of lurid romances.

Perfect. Though, if she wanted to fall asleep quickly, she might be better off with the book on how to build a proper castle.

Smiling to herself, Oleana pulled out a novel called *The Vicar's Daughter.*

Close enough.

"Those belonged to my wife."

She startled, the book sliding from her fingers and landing on her toe. She winced, peering into the darkness.

"Though I don't suppose she'll mind if you borrow one, Oleana." A quiet laugh met her ears. "Did you drop it on your foot? Well, I suppose that's better than tripping over one of the chairs or a table. I've been half-afraid you'd set your hair on fire with the way you're waving that lamp about."

He sounded…mild. Not annoyed. Or angry. Which was a vast improvement over the last time they'd spoken.

"My lord. I thought you were out for the evening."

"Hoped, I think you mean. And I was out this evening. At a ball, as it happens. Another overblown affair. There wasn't even decent punch being served."

"How unfortunate," she replied, feeling the awareness of Monteith's presence ripple over her skin. It was dangerous to be here, to be alone with him in the darkness. It felt far too intimate.

"Terribly. Do you know what it is like to be hunted, Mrs. Honeywell?"

Oddly enough, she did. "No, my lord."

"My friend Southwell once told me that if you were to toss in a piece of, say, chicken into one of the rivers of the Amazon, there is a fish there that will pick it clean to the bone in a matter of seconds. That's what tonight was like for me. Only, I didn't care for any of those fish."

"I take it you are the bit of chicken in the story. You've also compared yourself to a young lady beset upon by an unwelcome suitor."

A bark of quiet laughter came from him. "Ah yes. I seem the recipient of all sorts of unwanted affection."

Oleana looked away at his words, wishing she hadn't come to the library.

"I didn't mean yours, Oleana." The words were soft, pressing into her heart. "If you bear any for me."

She didn't answer, not willing to expose that part of herself. Raising the lamp, she caught just the outline of Montieth in the chair by the window. "It is odd to find you here, my lord."

"It's my bloody house."

She stepped closer even though she should keep her distance, pulled in his direction by unseen forces until the lamp bathed him with golden light. He was still in his evening clothes, but he'd taken off his cravat and coat.

"I haven't forgotten, my lord."

A low sound came from him. "I should like it if you called me Jason. Given what has occurred between us, I would prefer you use my Christian name rather than Montieth or 'my lord.' Seems somewhat formal, don't you think?" He ran a hand through the close-cropped waves of his hair. "We should talk about what happened, Oleana."

He'd flung her away from him because she was a member of his staff and he was an earl. Being with her infringed upon his honor. They could have nothing together but a discreet affair. Oleana understood; it was her heart that didn't wish to comply. "It isn't necessary."

"But it is. I insist. Come sit with me." He reached out a hand. "I will admit to you I've done nothing but think about you and that night. And also confess that is why I didn't care for any of the fish swimming about the pond I found myself in tonight. Hunt of all people," he said more to himself than her, "as it turns out, is possessed of a great deal of intelligence."

"Hunt?" Oleana took his hand before she could stop herself, her fingers curling around his. Montieth was warm, smelling of clean male with a hint of scotch.

"A friend. Far wiser than I am."

"Monteith—"

"Jason," he countered.

"I should go," she whispered as he pulled her closer, tilting the lamp.

"Give me that." He took the lamp with his other hand and placed it on the table. "Are you trying to set yourself and me on fire?"

I'm already on fire.

He pulled her into his lap, settling her against his thighs. A very distinctive hardness pressed into her backside. "Ignore that for the time being. Happens every time you're near me. I've grown used to it." Montieth waved his free hand. The other held her in a firm grip.

"I'll do my best. And try not to wiggle about overmuch." Oleana's feelings for this man were so brilliantly clear at the moment, in a way they hadn't been before.

His lips tilted upward as a smile broke across his handsome, usually stern features.

Oleana's breath caught. How...*stunning* he was when he smiled. Like the sun peeking through the clouds after days of rain. Her heart tripped over itself, beating about wildly in her chest. Before she could stop herself, Oleana ran her forefinger over the crease of his lips. "You should smile more often."

"I've had little reason to do so before you," he breathed, nipping at her finger. "My father was infamous for tupping the help, as I'm sure you know."

"Mrs. Beesom told me," she admitted.

He nodded. "It isn't any great secret, only something I've always told myself I would never do. I—" He looked away from her for a moment. "Well, that isn't what this is."

Her heart fluttered once more in his direction. "No, it is not.

But I am your housekeeper."

"No, you aren't. I think we can both drop that pretense right now." He didn't seem upset, only curious. "I will assume that your reasons for pretending to be one are—"

"I'm no one nefarious," she interrupted. "Not a criminal. I haven't wanted to...bend the truth, but it has been necessary." Oleana lifted her chin. "My affection for Elizabeth is real."

"And what about your affection for me?" He toyed with one of her curls, which had fallen to her cheek. "Is that real as well, Oleana?"

"Yes," she whispered. She threaded her fingers through the dark silk of his hair, tugging on the short strands before pulling his mouth to hers. "Very real." It was wrong, she knew, to distract him from whatever he wanted to discuss, but Oleana didn't want the Caraways to invade this small space with her and Monteith.

A groan left him as he yanked her closer, crushing her breasts against his chest. His mouth slanted more fully over hers in a heady merging of their lips that took her breath away. Oleana whimpered, pushing herself tightly into his body.

"I had every intention of only talking to you," he said against her mouth. "We must decide how we will—"

Oleana slid the tip of her tongue into his mouth, cutting him off. He would ask her to be his mistress, and Oleana wasn't sure what her answer would be. Or if she could share him with a wife.

I don't want to decide. Even if selling her father's farm made her wealthy, she was still no more than a vicar's widow. Still beneath him.

"Damn it, Oleana." His breathing became ragged against her throat. "You've managed to destroy all my good intentions." One big hand cupped her breast through the fabric of her dress. "Take this off," he commanded. "Or I might tear it from you."

"Yes." Oleana pushed him back and stood, unbuttoning the front of her simple gray dress. She wore only her chemise beneath it. Such a shapeless garment didn't require a corset.

Montieth stood with her, his fingers tracing hers as they

moved over the buttons. His teeth grazed the lobe of her ear. "I would have you wear silk the color of the ocean, Oleana. To match your eyes."

"Hardly practical for a housekeeper." She inhaled sharply as his mouth trailed over her shoulder.

"But not my—"

Another press of her mouth to his cut off the words she wasn't ready to hear. "Mistress" was what he would say. The cool air brushed over her skin as the dress and her lone petticoat dropped to the floor.

Jason stood, one hand glancing over her breast, his thumb circling around the sensitive peak of her nipple through the chemise. His hand reached up into her hair, pulling free the copper curls, pins flying over the floor. Another groan left him as his fingers threaded through the thick locks.

"*Jesus*, you're beautiful. And mine."

"Yes," she whispered. At least for now. Oleana knew in her heart their relationship couldn't continue past tonight. She didn't think she could be his mistress. Or even the wealthy widow he visited on occasion. Eventually she would hate him for it.

But she could have tonight. Have this. Just as she had the night in the kitchen.

Jason tore at her chemise, ripping the cotton until it hung from her. "I'll buy you dozens." The warmth of his mouth sucking at the peak of one nipple drove all the painful thoughts from her mind. She tore at his waistcoat as his hand slid down between her thighs, his fingers tangling in the hair of her mound.

He slid out of his waistcoat, then his shirt, pausing only to kiss her, until finally he flung both garments to the floor. When he was as naked as she was, save her hose, Jason cupped the side of her face with his hand.

"Mine," he said again, his tongue lapping at the corner of her mouth. He nudged her toward the sofa, and Oleana went gladly, lying down and opening her arms to him.

"I must do this properly one day. I long to have you in my

bed." He wrapped a handful of curls around his wrist, pinning her in place. Lifting her knee with his other hand, Jason settled between her thighs. He pressed a hard kiss to her mouth before thrusting his cock deep inside her with little warning.

Oleana gasped at the stretch as he filled her, tilting up her hips to take him deeper, watching the sinuous movement of his body as he took her in long, deep strokes. Her nails sank into the hard muscle of his buttocks, pulling him closer. Looking up at his handsome face, Oleana knew in her heart why she must leave. It would be easier for both of them. For Elizabeth too.

I love you. Her heart whispered the words she forbade her lips to repeat.

Jason twisted his body, catching hers, his eyes never leaving her face.

The movement drew her body tight, teasing her sensitive flesh, pushing her closer to release.

"There, my love?"

"Yes," she whimpered. She hooked her arms around his neck, never looking away, wanting to remember every moment of this night, pleasure etched sharply against her skin, her body tensing and curling around his. "Please, Jason."

"Not yet." He slowed again, pressing the heat of his mouth down her neck, his hand lowering to toy with her breast, rolling the nipple between his fingers before pinching the peak taut.

Oleana moaned loudly at the sharp sting, the sensation pulsing down between her thighs. He pulled back, thrusting hard into her with another twist of his hips. She arched against him, feeling his hand move around her throat. Pinning her against the leather of the sofa. The springs beneath them squeaked in protest as he ravished her.

Pleasure inched up her spine, the backs of her legs, across her breasts. Every stroke took her closer to the bliss she sought. His body caught against hers once more, and Oleana's entire world split apart. She clung to him, her legs straining around his hips as her release peaked sharply, unable to breathe or even think.

"Oleana." His large body covered hers. He took her faster, harder. "Mine," he whispered, burying himself deep inside her, his own breathing ragged and uneven before he stilled.

"Yes." She clasped him firmly to her heart, a tear sliding from one eye, wishing more than anything it could be true.

CHAPTER FIFTEEN

T HE NEXT MORNING, Oleana awoke, stretching her arms out, aware of the blissful soreness between her thighs. They'd lain together on the sofa in the library for hours afterward, talking and making love once more. He'd made her no promises, nor had he questioned her further about what had brought her to his household. Both of which she was grateful for. Nor had they discussed his future engagement to Miss Langham, an announcement Oleana expected any day. Instead, she'd enjoyed his warmth, his heart beating beneath her ear, and the happiness of knowing he cared for her.

She got out of bed, splashed water on her face, and quickly twisted her hair into a chignon at the back of her neck. Dressed, she stood and looked around the room for Carrot. She'd completely forgotten about him. How alarming. She got on her knees, looking under the bed.

Drat.

Carrot was gone. He must have slipped out last night when she'd returned from the library. It had been late. She'd been sleepy and still in a state of bliss. Carrot must have snuck past her in the dark. Well, there was no help for it, she'd have to go in search of the cat.

Flinging open the door, she was surprised to see Wilbert standing just outside, a smug tilt to his lips.

"Your presence is requested. Lord Montieth wants to see you

in his study. Immediately."

Oleana sailed past the butler. There were quite a lot of reasons Jason would summon her to his study before she'd even had breakfast. Perhaps he'd come to the same conclusion she had, that as wonderful as last night had been, Oleana must leave his household. Or perhaps he would tell her he meant to marry Miss Langham. Any other reason for her summons would likely be as unpleasant. Carrot *was* missing.

Nodding to herself, Oleana marched down the stairs, Wilbert at her heels. Once they arrived at Monteith's study, the butler knocked softly and opened the door. "Mrs. Honeywell, as you requested, my lord."

His back was to her, the man seemingly absorbed in something outside the window. Carrot was sitting atop his desk, tail flopping back and forth lazily. The cat gave Oleana a bland look as she entered.

Damn.

Wilbert noticed her discomfort. A sneer crossed his thin lips. "Tick tock," he whispered for her ears alone.

"Leave us, Wilbert," Montieth said without turning. "I need to have yet another very pointed discussion with Mrs. Honeywell. Please shut the door."

"Of course, my lord." Wilbert gave her another look, barely able to conceal his hopefulness that she would *finally* be dismissed.

The door shut behind the butler, but still, Jason didn't turn around. It was difficult to discern his mood merely from the top of his head and the hint of broad shoulders visible above the back of the chair.

"My lord—" she started, determined to tell him it would be best for both of them if she left at the end of the week. She'd been thinking of it for some time, after all. Mr. Hughes would likely send her a message today or tomorrow. She would wait until she had word, then secure other, temporary lodgings for herself and Carrot. Whatever offer Mr. Hughes made her for the farm,

Oleana would take. Find herself a cottage by the sea. A place where she'd never have to see the Earl and Countess of Montieth together.

"Come here, Oleana." His voice was soft, barely above a whisper.

She walked toward the desk. He didn't sound angry, exactly.

Montieth turned and faced her, his eyes dark as pewter and just as unreadable. Perhaps he was upset about Carrot. The cat *was* lying atop the middle stack of papers on the desk. Oleana reached out to pick up Carrot but was stopped.

"Leave the cat." Montieth stood swiftly and took hold of her shoulders. His mouth descended on hers. Hungry and hot. There was desperation in the claiming of her mouth. Possessiveness.

Longing.

Oleana sagged against him, powerless to resist him. Her fingers immediately curled into the fabric of his coat. She nipped at his bottom lip before gently lapping at his tongue with hers.

He groaned, one hand circling her neck.

At that moment, nothing in the world could have made her leave him.

"Turn," he said in a rough voice, his mouth leaving hers. Big hands squeezed her hips.

Moisture seeped between her thighs, her nipples tightening painfully beneath the plain wool of her dress as she faced the desk.

He nuzzled the back of her neck, his teeth grazing her skin. "Put your hands on the desk."

"Your papers," she stuttered, knowing what he meant to do. Wanting it.

"I don't give a fuck about the papers, Oleana."

She blushed at the curse, placing her palms flat on the desk. Her back arched against the warm hand trailing down the length of her spine. The same hand moved lower, pulling at her skirts, lifting them until the backs of her legs and buttocks were exposed.

"Lovely." Montieth ran one hand down her leg while the

other fell to the back of her neck, pressing her head gently to the desk. "I've thought of doing this"—his other hand found its way to the already wet flesh between her thighs—"for quite some time."

A low whimper came from her as his forefinger traced around her opening.

"Why do you think I called you to my study so often? Every time you appeared, I imagined you on this desk, my hips or my head between your thighs." She heard him fumble with his clothing as his fingers left her. A kiss was pressed on the plump cheek of one buttock. "You've a beautiful backside, Oleana. I plan to spend entire evenings admiring it."

Her eyelids fluttered closed as she refused to allow herself the luxury of considering a future with Montieth. He held the lower half of her body up, his other hand still wrapped around her neck as he entered her with exquisite slowness.

She moaned, pushing back her hips, trying to compel him to sink deeper.

"Greedy," he whispered along the line of her back.

"Yes," she whimpered as he seated himself. The angle hit a particularly sensitive spot inside her. "Don't be gentle," she begged. "I don't need you to be."

Montieth groaned, pounding into her until the pleasure was so intense she bit her lip to keep from screaming out. Papers fluttered from the desk onto the floor. Pens scattered. Belatedly, Oleana realized the window behind them was open to the street. Dear God, someone walking by could see them. The thought caused her pleasure to peak sharply, and she clawed at the desk.

His hand moved from her throat to her lips, the earl silencing Oleana as she screamed out her release.

"Quiet now." Montieth groaned at the pull of her body against his. He laced their fingers together as he thrust once more, his head falling to her back as he climaxed.

Panting, dizzy with pleasure, Oleana opened her eyes to see Carrot calmly cleaning himself.

A stupid grin pulled at her lips. That had been bloody marvelous.

"Oleana." Montieth kissed the side of her cheek. "Did I hurt you, sweetheart? I'm sorry. I should have at least wished you good morning before falling on you like a rabid animal. I've done that repeatedly. Ravished you like some savage." He pressed his lips to her cheek again. "I'm sorry."

"No." She squeezed his fingers. "It was a pleasant surprise. Much better than the eggs I was going to have for breakfast."

Monteith chuckled. "Carrot doesn't seem impressed."

Oleana started to giggle. Snorted.

Montieth laughed louder, shaking her body still trapped beneath his.

Why must she love a man she couldn't have? This man? What irony to know she'd agonized over wedding Percival because she thought him so far above her. And Monteith—

"Am I forgiven for my unprovoked attack?" he teased as he slowly pulled away from her.

"You are absolutely forgiven, though I do wish you'd thought to shut the drapes. I'm grateful the gardener isn't trimming the hedges around the windows today."

Another deep, rumbling sound came from him. Beautiful. Melodious.

"I love to hear you laugh, my lord."

He lowered her skirts, taking his time smoothing the plain gray wool down her legs. "I never thought it so easy to do. You make me happier than I have been...well, in a very long time."

His arms came around her waist, the earl embracing her, his cheek against her back. Turning her to face him, he moved to stand between her thighs, cupping her face in his big hands. "Lovely creature. I quite adore you."

A knock sounded at the door, and Oleana jumped away from Montieth, moving swiftly to the bookcases. She bent down, pretending to look for something underneath the sofa.

"What is it, Wilbert?" Montieth asked.

The butler pranced into the study, never once glancing in

Oleana's direction. She wasn't even sure he knew she was still here.

"Lady Langham and her daughter have arrived, my lord. I put them in the drawing room. Tea will arrive in a moment."

"Thank you, Wilbert."

"May I say, my lord, how happy the staff are for your upcoming announcement concerning Miss Langham? We are quite thrilled."

A disgruntled noise came from Montieth. "Thank you, Wilbert. I'll be a moment."

Oleana tightened her hands on the rug, waiting for the wave of pain to leave her. Hadn't she agonized over this very subject last night after they'd made love? She knew Montieth had to marry. If not Miss Langham, then some other flower of society. He needed an heir.

Her hand fell to her midsection. A son was something Oleana couldn't give him even if things were different. She'd never conceived with Percival. She was likely barren.

"Oleana." Monteith peered at her from beneath the sofa on the other side. "You can come out now."

She managed to stand without bumping her head and took hold of the bottom of the sofa while she came to her feet, careful to keep her features composed. "I should go, my lord. Ensure the tea tray is properly sorted out."

He reached for her, and she evaded him, bumping her hip on a table as she did so.

"We will speak later, Oleana. There are things we need to discuss, without distractions," he murmured in a low tone, a frown fixed on his lips.

"Of course, my lord." She turned and hurried off to the safety of her room. Wilbert and Mrs. Beesom would see to the tea tray. Oleana wasn't in the mood to worry about whether Miss Langham enjoyed her bloody scones at the moment.

I have to leave.

She did. She'd known from the moment they'd first touched each other in the kitchen. Dragging her valise out from under the bed, Oleana wiped away a tear threatening to spill from her eyes. Elizabeth would think she'd been abandoned. That was what hurt most. But Oleana could hardly stay and watch the man she loved—

Love. I love Jason. So much.

—marry another woman. Nor could she continue to be his housekeeper under the circumstances. She certainly couldn't agree to be his mistress. It was simply time to go. She turned toward her bed for the familiar ball of orange fur, intent on pouring out her misery to Carrot, before remembering he'd been in the study when she and Montieth had—

Heat flooded up her cheeks at the remembrance of what had occurred only a short time ago.

The first order of business was to find Carrot, then put all thoughts of Montieth ravishing her over his desk out of her mind. And forget about Miss Langham sitting in the drawing room. Oleana could simply go to the train station tonight and buy a ticket to *somewhere*. Write to Mr. Hughes wherever she landed. A brilliant plan.

Marching out of her room, she made her way back to the study. Carrot was probably under Montieth's desk or hiding in the bookshelves.

"There you are, Mrs. Honeywell. Always lurking about, aren't you?" Wilbert stood watching her, his hands clasped behind his back.

"I'm looking for Carrot." She brushed past him. "Lord Monteith has asked that I put him in my room while he has callers."

"A brilliant idea. I believe he's in the kitchen. Mrs. Beesom has a bit of chicken left over from the stock she's making. She offered some to the beast, though I'm not sure why." His lip curled. "You'd best fetch him before he ends up outside the drawing room, Mrs. Honeywell. Or somewhere equally disastrous." He started toward the kitchen. "And I'm not touching that cat."

"Good." Oleana turned and followed Wilbert to the kitchen, sticking out her tongue once his back was turned.

CHAPTER SIXTEEN

J ASON POURED HIMSELF a scotch from the sideboard and settled himself on the sofa in his study. Yesterday's visit with Miss Langham and her mother had been incredibly awkward as the two women waited impatiently for Jason to give a firm indication that he would call upon Lord Langham and offer for their daughter. Instead, Jason had gone to his club to dine last night knowing Langham would probably arrive at some point, and he had. Jason had made it clear to Langham that he wouldn't be offering for Miss Jane Langham, though she was a lovely girl.

Marrying Miss Langham was the dutiful thing to do. But Jason's heart wasn't on duty or honor or the glory of the bloody earldom. Every time Lady Langham had dropped a careful hint yesterday at tea, a vision of Oleana and Elizabeth holding hands while taking a moon bath had flashed before him. It was the most beautiful scene he could imagine: the two beings he loved best in the world.

Yes, love. There was hardly any point in denying it.

He'd arrived home from his club late and gone up to bed, half considering seeking out Oleana, not to coax her into his bed, though that certainly would have been wonderful, but because he simply wanted to talk to her. He needed to tell her he had no intention of marrying Jane Langham. Or any of the other young ladies his mother had suggested. Jason needed to tell her it didn't matter what complications had brought her to his door. They would sort things out. Together. Oleana needed to know what was in his heart.

Jason meant to tell her today.

He'd arisen late and come down to his study to work, finding himself behind without Mathers here. Carrot joined him, slinking through the door when Jason wasn't looking and padding over to the desk. A large orange blob was now resting on the invitations Jason had no inclination to attend. It was a credit to how happy Jason found himself and how sure he was about his feelings for Oleana that he merely scratched the big cat behind the ears.

"My lord." Jones, the secretary Jason didn't like as much as Mathers, stood at the entrance to the study. "Apologies for disturbing you, but this just arrived. Urgent, I expect. From Mathers." Jones held a letter in one sweaty hand.

Another reason not to like Jones besides his poor filing abilities: the man seemed constantly clammy. He left moisture on everything.

Jason nodded and took the letter from Jones, dismissing the young man with a wave. After breaking the seal, he read the perfectly precise handwriting of Mathers, something else Jones should learn to emulate.

After searching Shropshire thoroughly, I ascertained that Mrs. Honeywell was indeed your aunt's housekeeper. However, it is not the Mrs. Honeywell currently employed by you in London.

Well, that wasn't really much of a surprise. Jason had long suspected Oleana wasn't really a housekeeper. She'd admitted as much to him the other night.

The Mrs. Honeywell employed by your aunt had a grand-daughter who visited her on occasion. The description of the granddaughter, short of stature with a full head of flaming red hair, certainly sounds like your Mrs. Honeywell, my lord.

She was his Mrs. Honeywell, wasn't she?

KATHLEEN AYERS

Jason tried to ignore the pleasure the thought gave him and failed miserably. Oleana was his. And he belonged to her.

The information Mathers had uncovered in Shropshire made a great deal of sense. Oleana knew quite a bit about his great-aunt's home and the surrounding area. Jason had already decided she must be the relative of one of his aunt's previous staff, who'd seen an opportunity to escape the remote village of Badger and venture to London. He'd been to Badger. He couldn't blame her for wanting to leave.

> The trail of the two Mrs. Honeywells led me from Shropshire to a village outside of Shrewsbury named Picklescott, notable only for it being the home of Lord Delacorte. After several careful inquiries, I learned that Mrs. Honeywell's description matched that of a vicar's widow who disappeared from the area some months ago.

"She's a vicar's widow," Jason said out loud to the empty room before returning to Mathers's letter, ignoring the slight unease starting to settle in his chest.

> Her dead husband's family has been searching for her. Theft of some valuable heirloom is the reason. Some people in Picklescott think she might have taken something from the vicarage because Delacorte is involved in the search. The vicarage sits at the edge of his estate. Everyone I spoke to described your Mrs. Honeywell, right down to her propensity to running into any object in the vicinity.

Oleana a thief? Jason refused to believe such a thing. She'd confessed to him that her masquerade as a housekeeper didn't involve anything nefarious.

> There's a bit more. The gossip, which I heard in the pub, is that Mrs. Honeywell might have caused her husband's death. He fell off his horse while riding home one night after tending to one of his flock, and some have speculated Mrs. Honeywell

deliberately jumped out at him in the darkness. Apparently, the vicar had a weak heart.

Not just a thief but a murderess? Jason set the letter down and went to the sideboard to pour himself another drink. After a swallow of scotch, he picked up the letter again, a sickening feeling of disbelief clouding his thoughts.

Had she deliberately lied to him? Had he fallen in love with a criminal?

The tales I heard paint a picture of unlawful behavior. However, there are several facts that don't quite make sense to me, my lord. I continue to investigate. My next quarry is the late vicar's family. I sense something is not completely right.

Jason folded up the letter and put it back in his pocket. Mathers had neglected to give him the name of the vicar's family—an oversight. Still, his secretary had done an outstanding job in searching out the mystery that was Oleana. The very idea that she was a criminal and possible murderess was ridiculous in Jason's mind. He considered himself a fairly good judge of character.

Yes, but you were wrong about me, the voice of Alice, his dead wife, whispered against his ear.

Jason swallowed the rest of his scotch, refilled the glass, and plopped back down on the sofa. He hadn't loved Alice, but he had thought her honorable, decent. He'd been wrong on both counts. Alice hadn't been a maid when they'd wed, nor had she honored their agreement that she stay faithful to him long enough to produce an heir. She'd given Jason Elizabeth, then had promptly gone back to fucking her cousin and lied to Jason about it. Alice had been with child when she'd died, but Jason had known it wasn't his. He hadn't touched her for nearly a year before her death.

"Yes, I'm a bloody great judge of character." He swallowed the amber liquid, letting it burn down his throat. There was every chance, based on the report Mathers had sent, that he was wrong about Oleana as well. Had he spent the entire previous evening actually considering marriage—

He stood, setting his glass down on the table so hard he nearly shattered the crystal. It was time Mrs. Honeywell gave up her secrets. He would hear them all. Now.

Walking out into the hall, he caught Jones speaking to Bessie, the young maid who often helped with Elizabeth. "Bessie, have you seen Mrs. Honeywell?" His fingers twitched impatiently against his thigh. "I need to discuss the dinner menu with her." Jason had never so much as talked about a potato with Oleana, but Bessie didn't know that.

The girl blushed at his attention before coming forward. "No, my lord." Confusion wrinkled her brow. "Apologies, my lord, but Mrs. Honeywell isn't...*here* any longer."

Jason's fingers stilled. "Excuse me?"

Bessie's cheeks reddened further. "I—assumed you knew, my lord. Mrs. Honeywell resigned her position." She looked to Jones for help, who as usual, had sweat gathering on his upper lip.

Jones nodded. "Mr. Wilbert made the announcement to the staff yesterday, my lord. Mrs. Honeywell resigned." He cleared his throat. "When you summoned her to your study yesterday, we—that is, the staff—well, we thought you knew."

There was a great deal that had happened in his study, but never had there been a discussion of Oleana *leaving* him.

Yes, him. The feeling of betrayal was enormous. Almost as bad as the possibility she was a vicar's widow involved in thievery and murder.

"Where can I find Wilbert?" His butler had not seen fit to inform Jason, which was unacceptable. Oleana had been gone for almost an entire day, and Jason hadn't known. More pain stretched across his heart.

"In the kitchen, my lord." Bessie glanced up at him with fear-filled eyes.

Jason took off in the direction of the kitchen, finding Wilbert hovering about the hall, dictating to two maids who apparently hadn't made Jason's bed to his satisfaction.

Jason had had no idea he was so picky.

"Wilbert, a word, if you please."

"My lord." The priggish butler came forward with a bow. "How may I be of service?"

"I understand Mrs. Honeywell resigned her position yesterday."

"Indeed, my lord. In a manner of speaking." Wilbert's eyes shifted away from Jason. "I would not say so much a resignation as purging your home of dishonesty." The butler's tone took on a self-righteous edge. "Her husband's brother came to fetch her and bring her back to her family. Her name isn't even Mrs. Honeywell." Wilbert puffed out his chest. "She's a thief, my lord. Stole from a kind family who took her in after she wed her son. Once she became a widow, she repaid them by absconding with valuables belonging to them. I knew her letter of recommendation was false. She had not one bit of skill at managing a house." Wilbert held up the keys Oleana had worn at her waist but rarely used. "There was no time to pack her things, as Mr. Parkworth wished to set off immediately." Wilbert frowned. "Though, I was not given a forwarding address."

"Mr. Parkworth?" He felt like strangling Wilbert.

"Yes, as I said, he is her husband's brother." Wilbert leaned in so his voice was barely above a whisper. "There is conjecture, according to Mr. Parkworth, that she may have hurried along her husband's demise." He straightened. "I acted immediately, of course, in handing her over as my position and duty dictates. She was not pleased at all, my lord, at being caught. Struggled something fierce. But I had two of the footmen assist Mr. Parkworth in putting her in the carriage." Wilbert smiled, awaiting Jason's praise for ridding his household of the problem of Mrs. Honeywell.

He should fire Wilbert this instant. Oleana hadn't resigned her position. She hadn't left him. She'd been forcibly removed from his home while Jason had been sipping tea with Miss Langham. Whether she was deceitful wasn't up to his bloody butler but to Jason.

"Mr. Wilbert, might I ask how you knew this Mr. Parkworth wasn't lying?"

The butler flushed. "He had no reason to, my lord."

"Did Mr. Parkworth have a constable with him? Any proof at all of his claims?"

"Why, no," Wilbert stuttered. "But she knew Mr. Parkworth."

"You had my footmen force Mrs. Honeywell into a carriage with a man who gave you absolutely no proof of his identity and his claims. I should have been informed immediately of Mr. Parkworth's presence in my house. You should have come to me at once concerning Mrs. Honeywell. Instead, one of my maids had to tell me."

"She could be a murderess," Wilbert protested with a whine.

"You forget yourself, Wilbert. This is my household, not yours." Jason spun on his heel and strode away, ignoring the butler who was sniffing behind him. Jason found Jones where he'd left him. "A message must be sent to Mathers immediately, Jones."

"Yes, my lord." Jones nodded and hurried off to find a groom.

Oleana wasn't a murderer. Jason might not know everything about her, but he knew that much. If she had stolen something from her late husband's family, the Parkworths, why hadn't it been a constable who'd come for her instead of her brother-in-law?

Because a constable would have asked to speak to Jason.

Something was very wrong. Mathers thought so as well. Taking the stairs two at a time, Jason yelled for Entwistle, his valet. He needed to pack and leave for Shrewsbury. Tonight.

CHAPTER SEVENTEEN

O LEANA LOOKED OUT at the passing countryside, stretching her hands as far as she could with the rope around them. Never in her wildest imaginings had Oleana thought Mrs. Caraway would stoop to kidnapping. Though in retrospect, she should have guessed. Her former mother-in-law was greedy, possessed of the sort of grasping neediness that blotted out everything else. She was willing to force Oleana to marry Albert; why not resort to kidnapping?

When Wilbert had led her down to the kitchen yesterday, Oleana had been expecting to find Carrot making a nuisance of himself. But the moment she'd stepped into the warm space, usually bustling with staff, Oleana knew something was wrong. No one had been in the kitchen. Not Carrot. Not even Mrs. Beesom.

Only Albert Parkworth.

"Thief," Wilbert had hissed from behind her, blocking the stairs as Oleana tried to get away. "I always knew there was something suspicious about you. Now I know why."

"Hello, Oleana," Albert had drawled from the door at the back, the one used to take deliveries. He'd held a length of rope in his hands, snapping it absently against his thigh as he approached her. "Thank you, Mr. Wilbert, for helping me recover my errant sister-in-law. I'm sure you've surmised she's a bit teched in the head, what with stealing from her loving family and running away. We long to have her back with us." Menace and the promise of retribution had gleamed in Albert's dark eyes.

"I've stolen nothing." Terror had made her nearly faint. "Please, Wilbert. He's lying. They want my father's—" Albert had stuck a handkerchief in her mouth before grabbing her roughly and swiftly binding her wrists.

"You hush now, Oleana. You'll be home safe and sound very soon," Albert had whispered in her ear.

"Are you sure that's necessary, Mr. Parkworth?" Wilbert had said, barely glancing at Oleana.

She had stamped her foot, struggling to spit out the cloth in her mouth.

"Completely. You don't want her to start screaming, do you? Didn't you say the earl has callers? I'm sure you don't want him disturbed, not with such a sordid matter."

"No." Wilbert had stepped back at the reminder. He'd smoothed down the edges of his uniform, flicking away a piece of lint. "I do not."

Wilbert hadn't even been able to look at her as Albert pulled her out the door. The coward.

By now, the shock of Albert's appearance in Montieth's kitchen had started to wear off, but not her panic at being in his control. She glanced at the man sitting across from her in the rocking coach, fear seeping into her bones.

Albert Parkworth was the child of Mrs. Caraway and her first husband, a merchant from Shrewsbury. Older than Oleana's dead husband by some ten years, Albert was a thick, muscular man, his build more akin to that of a prizefighter than a gentleman. He was fleshy. Hairy. Thick. Percival had nicknamed him Bear. Albert was often sullen and brooding. There was little cheer in him, likely the result of always standing in Percival's shadow. Oleana had never liked him, nor the way his hooded eyes had followed her about when Percival was alive.

Albert caught her looking at him. "Remembering where you left the deed to your family farm, Oleana?" Albert said. "I looked under every bloody floorboard in your father's house. I even went to your grandmother's and searched as well. Where is it?"

There was some pleasure to be had in knowing she'd sent Albert on a wild goose chase across the countryside to search her grandmother's cottage for the deed to the farm. "I'm sorry you wasted your time looking for something that doesn't belong to you to begin with."

"We are owed something for keeping you fed and clothed all these years." He glowered at her.

"I was married to Percival," she replied, trying to keep her voice steady, "the wife of a vicar. I believe it is the patronage of Lord Delacorte and Percival's flock that kept us fed and clothed, not Mrs. Caraway and certainly not you."

"Mother and I see things differently, Oleana."

"The farm is mine," she said. "It was never part of my dowry."

"The farm belongs to Percival and thus Mother and me." Albert's eyes ran over her.

"Percival is dead," she answered. "He never wanted the farm. Your mother viewed it as merely a burden. A place to send me once I became widowed."

Albert shrugged. "Our opinion has changed." Albert leaned over and put a hand on her knee. "It will become mine once we wed."

"I am not marrying you," she whispered, shirking from his touch. "Percival would be horrified."

"Percival, as you've just pointed out, is dead. But even if he weren't, I don't think he'd mind me bedding you, Oleana. He lost interest in your charms some time ago. Said you were much too bold in the bedroom for his tastes. He liked his women a bit shier. And not barren. Lucky for you, I don't feel the same."

Oleana's stomach curdled at the thought of Albert in all his hairy fleshiness, touching her.

"Mr. Hughes won't buy the property without a proper deed. He said as much when he called upon your mother after

Percival's death," Oleana hissed. "And you won't have the deed even if you wed me, because I won't give it to you. One carefully raised suspicion, and Mr. Hughes will walk away from the deal. I'll say—"

"No one will listen to you, Oleana. Everyone is convinced you're unstable. Scaring Percival off his horse. Stealing from the family. Not to mention the rumors of your lascivious nature."

Oleana gritted her teeth. "None of that is true."

"Lord Delacorte thinks every word is true. So does most of the countryside, especially after Mother begged him to help find you. Your instability, you see, caused you to scare poor Percival off his horse, then you climbed into bed with me. Delacorte was absolutely horrified. He promised to help Mother in any way he could."

Another wave of nausea hit her. "It isn't true."

"Doesn't matter." Albert smacked his lips, his eyes straying to her bodice. "Once we sell the property to Mr. Hughes—and we will, make no mistake—there will be plenty of money to keep Mother and me for the rest of our lives in grand style. Even after we pay back Delacorte for his assistance. It was his man who found you in London, after all. But don't worry, we'll set aside a bit for the sanatorium in Leeds."

Bile rose in Oleana's throat. "Sanatorium?"

Albert shook his head regretfully. "We really don't have a choice about the sanatorium, Oleana. You'll only cause problems if we allow you to. Mother has already visited Leeds and assures me you'll be happy there. Once I've had my fill of you, that is." A slow, malicious grin crossed his thick lips. "Maybe if you hand over the deed and promise to behave, Mother will reconsider."

Oleana forced her eyes to the window and the passing countryside, trying not to throw up the small bit of bread she'd eaten earlier. The very idea of submitting to Albert or Mrs. Caraway sickened her. She had never felt so alone in her life, not even after her father had died. Wilbert would have told the staff by now that she was gone. What had he told Montieth? That she'd resigned her position or ran off?

Jason. Her heart sobbed his name.

How stubborn and foolish she'd been not to tell him about Mrs. Caraway. Montieth cared for her, housekeeper or not. He would have protected her. Now Oleana doubted he would look on her so kindly. Wilbert had probably told Montieth by now, branding her a thief, a possible murderess, and half out of her mind to boot. At the very least, Montieth would know she'd lied by not telling him about the Caraways. And Wilbert would have painted her in the worst light possible.

Oleana blinked back the moisture gathering in her eyes, refusing to give Albert the satisfaction of seeing her collapse into a fit of tears. She had to remain strong if she had any hope of getting out of the current situation.

Because no one would be coming for her. Oleana would have to save herself.

CHAPTER EIGHTEEN

M RS. CARAWAY'S LIPS curled in a brittle smile as Oleana was shoved into the drawing room by Albert. At least he'd untied her hands before they'd exited the carriage, though Oleana suspected it was only out of fear a neighbor or one of the servants might see.

Although, there didn't seem to be anyone about except Mrs. Caraway.

Rubbing her wrists, Oleana glanced around the drawing room. She'd hoped never to see this place or her former mother-in-law again. One look told Oleana exactly why Mrs. Caraway had resorted to kidnapping. The furnishings of the drawing room were sparse, not the lavish elegance Oleana remembered. At least two chairs were missing, as well as the painting over the fireplace. The main foyer was now absent of the magnificent Persian rug that had once graced the floor. Neglect and approaching poverty hung heavy in the air.

Mrs. Caraway had depended on Percival and the vicarage to support her for years. Albert, as far as Oleana knew, did nothing to contribute to the family's fortunes.

"There you are, Oleana." Mrs. Caraway's dark hair was pulled back from her temples so tightly the corners of her eyes stretched, giving her a vaguely feline appearance. Desperation had furrowed lines at the edges of her lips and across her brow, ruining her once smooth skin. As she was widowed twice, both of

Mrs. Caraway's husbands should have left her comfortable, but she wasn't the least frugal, spending lavishly on everything from clothing to furnishings and expensive cutlery. The vicarage and the patronage of Lord Delacorte had been the pinnacle of Mrs. Caraway's ambitions. Her son had been a respected vicar. Delacorte invited her often to dine with him. She'd walked around Picklescott like a queen, lording it over everyone else for years.

Now all that was gone.

If Oleana hadn't been forcibly abducted and brought here to be wed to Albert, she could almost feel some pity for her. Almost.

Mrs. Caraway studied Oleana as if she was some great oddity, her head tilted to one side. The fashionable olive silk gown edged in black lace rustled softly as she came forward. There may be no maids to clean the dust from the tables, or fine rugs left, but Mrs. Caraway refused to allow impoverishment to affect her wardrobe.

Albert pecked Mrs. Caraway's cheek in greeting. "Here she is, Mother. She still won't say what she's done with the deed."

"Maybe I tossed it in the fire." Oleana refused to behave like some trapped animal, though that was certainly how she felt. She was terrified and under the control of a woman who had long despised her.

"Don't think to threaten me, you ungrateful little twit," Mrs. Caraway said in a deceptively soft tone.

"You've kidnapped me. Threatened me. Made false accusations about me." Oleana shook her head. "But I'm not marrying Albert. You'll have to drag me, bound and gagged, to the vicar."

"Did I ever tell you, Oleana, how close Lord Delacorte and I are? After I explained to him about your strange behavior over the years, your raving in mindless abandon and your crude, obscene manner—why, he offered to help me find you immediately. Your clumsiness, I told him, was a sign of your illness. You were a danger to yourself and others. I suspected you'd gone to London to find Mr. Hughes." She leaned over. "And I was right."

Oleana sucked in a breath. "None one could possibly believe that of me."

"Oh, but they do. You see, Percival was a saint to endure your marriage, and you repaid him by deliberately frightening him off his horse." She gave a pout. "Grief at what you'd done thrust you into the arms of Albert. And he, out of respect for Percival, has offered to wed you and see to your welfare."

"How dare you paint me as some sort of a murderous light-skirts—"

"And thief," Mrs. Caraway added helpfully. "A woman unable to control her base urges. I'm afraid the gossip has been rather unfavorable to you, Oleana. If you are thinking there is anyone who would stop you from wedding Albert, you are sadly mistaken. I am doing you a favor, poor child. Not one person, not even Lord Delacorte, will be surprised when we have to send you to Leeds." Mrs. Caraway shot her a look of pity. "I assume Albert has informed you of the sanatorium? Lovely place. You'll be very happy there. No one in Leeds will believe you either."

"You can't do this." Her mind reeled at Mrs. Caraway's plans for her.

"I already have, Oleana," she replied in a smug tone. "You aren't really that intelligent. Oh, yes, you can grow beans—" A laugh like broken glass erupted from her. "—and entertain children, but when it comes to true intelligence, you are woefully lacking. Your ridiculous flight to London, for example. All you did was delay the inevitable."

No. This couldn't be happening. Panic and horror mixed inside her, making her unsteady on her feet. "When Lord Montieth finds out you've forcibly taken me from his residence—"

"Nonsense." Mrs. Caraway batted a hand in Oleana's direction. "You were a terrible housekeeper, and Montieth's butler—" She paused, snapping her fingers in Albert's direction.

"Mr. Wilbert," he supplied.

"Yes, Mr. Wilbert was only too happy to assist Lord Delacorte's man and then Albert. We've known where you were for weeks now. It wasn't hard to convince Wilbert you were some sort of criminal. Of his own accord, he even searched your room for evidence, though unfortunately, no deed was found."

Oleana's fists clenched. Wilbert. All this time, he'd been helping Mrs. Caraway. He had no idea what he'd done.

"Pity, because I might have been able to convince Mr. Hughes with only that piece of paper, saving us all a great deal of trouble. Ah, well." Mrs. Caraway threw her hands up in the air. "I'll have a wedding to be *very* sure the farm comes to us. I'd hate for Mr. Hughes to question our honesty." A thin finger wagged in Oleana's face. "You won't be escaping this time. Where are her things, Albert?"

"Mr. Wilbert assured me he searched her room himself. Nothing but some clothes and a book or two. The earl was entertaining guests, and Mr. Wilbert didn't want the disruption of bringing her things down. I told him I'd send for them later or collect them myself."

Mrs. Caraway's mouth pursed. "But not until after the wedding. And leave that atrocious cat. I don't want that creature near me again."

"Not to worry, Mother. Mr. Wilbert assured me he meant to get rid of the cat." Albert smiled at Oleana. "Bye-bye, Carrot."

"No." Oleana's voice trembled at her thinking of poor Carrot hurt or hungry, with no one to love him. Montieth didn't like Carrot, but surely he wouldn't allow Wilbert to dispose of an innocent animal? "I won't do it!" she yelled. "I won't marry Albert. He's my dead husband's stepbrother. No vicar in his right mind would agree to this—"

Albert grabbed her by her hair, cutting off the rest of her words. He jerked her head back, forcing her to her knees in front of Mrs. Caraway. "There will be no more of that, Oleana." He tugged at the strands of her hair until Oleana cried out in pain. "We may have to drug her for the ceremony, Mother."

"She's delusional." Mrs. Caraway's jaw hardened. "I'll let Vicar Thompson know how badly her mental state has deteriorated, that she's far worse than we suspected. I'll remind him again of the sacrifice you're making, Albert. And I've already gotten permission, Oleana, for you to wed Albert, though I'm not sure it was necessary. Albert and Percival weren't related by blood, if you'll recall. I merely reminded the bishop of the fact.

"But it isn't right." Oleana shut her eyes against the sting of her hair being ripped out by Albert's large, hairy hands. "I won't—"

Mrs. Caraway slapped Oleana so hard her head snapped to the side. "Look, you troublesome girl. I have had quite enough of your mouth. Now, where is the deed? We searched your grandmother's home. It isn't at Montieth's, if that butler is to be believed. I tore apart that hovel you once called home. There were mice droppings, Oleana." She bent down to look into Oleana's face. "I even questioned your father's ancient solicitor. Where. Is. It?

"You two would be terrible at a scavenger hunt. Remind me never to partner with you," Oleana snapped back.

Her mother-in-law's palm cracked against her cheek once more, this time drawing blood at the corner of Oleana's mouth.

"I never liked you, Oleana," Mrs. Caraway spat. "A farmer's daughter wasn't nearly good enough for my Percival, yet I welcomed you into my home. Treated you like a daughter—"

Blood dribbled down Oleana's chin as she snorted in derision.

"We are the only family you have, Oleana. I *will* have that property. I *will* sell to Mr. Hughes. No misbegotten trollop who was once married to my son is going to stop me."

Mrs. Caraway was the one who belonged in the sanatorium. Her greed had driven her insane.

"You're mad."

Mrs. Caraway's lip curled. "So stubborn," she hissed. "Do you know how hard I have worked to make this all come to fruition? Vicar Thompson balked at wedding a young lady who might not be in her right mind, but I convinced him it was for the best. Do you know how difficult this has been for me, Oleana? I'm still grieving for Percival, and you are so *selfish* you can't just do as you're told as any dumb animal would. No one cares what happens to you, Oleana, something you'll find out soon enough when I send you to the sanatorium."

"Lord Montieth—"

"Stupid girl. You were only his housekeeper for a short time. Montieth has probably forgotten by now you even existed. Do you really think he'd look for a runaway servant?"

Oleana thought she might be ill all over Mrs. Caraway's expensive olive silk skirts. Her mother-in-law was right. No one would stop her marriage to Albert.

"Albert, dear." Mrs. Caraway turned. "Would you escort our sweet Oleana up to her rooms? It will allow you two a chance to talk. You're going to be married, after all." She dismissed them both with a wave.

Albert leered at Oleana, pulling her up by her hair until she stood before him. "Come along, then." He half dragged her up the stairs, not pausing when she stumbled on the steps. He pulled her down the wooden floor of the hallway to a room at the far end. She struggled against him as he pushed her inside, gasping when Albert's hand grabbed at one of her breasts, squeezing until she cried out at the pain.

"Full of fire. Keep fighting, Oleana. It only makes me want you more." He pushed his hips against hers until Oleana felt the truth of his words. "But I'm not allowed until we're wed. Mother insists it isn't proper."

Hysterical laughter tried to bubble up her throat. Maybe she had lost her mind. "But forcing me to wed you and kidnapping me to steal my father's farm is acceptable?"

"Just give her the deed, Oleana. We could have a proper marriage if you'd just accept things. I don't care that you're barren." He leered at her. "What use do I have for a passel of brats?"

Albert tugged her roughly to his chest and pressed a slobbering kiss to her mouth.

Oleana slapped at him, scratching and punching as she struggled to break free. Her nails clawed at his face, drawing blood, and he released her with a curse. He tossed her to the floor, kicking her with the toe of his boot, his free hand pressed to his bleeding cheek.

"I would rather," she hissed, "go to the sanatorium."

"Suit yourself." An ugly look crossed his face. "But we'll have some fun before you go." He slammed the door shut behind him, the click of the lock loud in the quiet room.

Oleana drew in a breath, horrified at what her future would hold if she didn't manage to escape the Caraway house. She ran to the windows, but they'd all been nailed shut. She pounded on the locked door, screaming to be released, hoping a maid might hear her, but gave up when she remembered there was no sign of any servants in the house. Even if she still employed a housekeeper or cook, Mrs. Caraway wouldn't be so foolish as to have anyone here when Albert arrived with Oleana.

Falling into a heap on the floor, Oleana hugged her knees to her chest, trying hard not to weep with despair now that she was alone. Mrs. Caraway and Albert were convinced the deed to her father's land was either here or at her grandmother's cottage, but it was safe in London. Wilbert wasn't as thorough as he'd told them. It might be the only advantage she had, and it wasn't really much of one. Once Albert married her, she knew Mrs. Caraway would find a way to convince her father's solicitor to turn over the farm so she could sell to Mr. Hughes.

Elizabeth was due back from her visit with Lady Trent next week. What would she do when she returned home and found Oleana gone? And what about poor Carrot? Was he, even now, out on the streets, alone?

Jason.

Oleana wrapped her arms tight around her stomach, wishing she could go back to that morning in his study. How she wished she'd told him everything. Now he would think the worst of her, maybe be glad she was gone. And she was hopelessly trapped.

With a sob, she collapsed, pressing her face into the floor.

CHAPTER NINETEEN

"**M**Y LORD."

Jason looked up as Mathers came through the doors of the rooms they'd rented in Picklescott. Jason had arrived late last night after a delayed start to his journey to this small village outside Shrewsbury. The day he'd received the letter from Mathers and then found Oleana had been taken, Jason had packed his bags, ready to leave immediately, but a sudden thunderstorm had delayed his departure until the following morning. He'd decided at the last minute not to take his coach but to come on horseback, an urgent voice inside him insisting time was of the essence. Horseback was quicker.

Luckily, the note he'd sent ahead had found Mathers, who in turn had secured these rooms for Jason upon his arrival. He'd wanted to immediately go in search of Oleana, but Mathers had convinced Jason of the wisdom of a bit of rest, a bath, and food before setting out.

The lodgings Mathers had taken for Jason were sparsely furnished but clean. The food was decent, his bath lukewarm. But none of that mattered, because he needed to find Oleana. Now.

"Hello, Mathers," he greeted his secretary.

"There's a farm, my lord," Mathers blurted out. "And the dead vicar's name is Caraway, not Parkworth."

Jason raised a brow. He'd told Mathers what had happened to Oleana and about Parkworth's arrival. "Caraway? Then who is

Albert Parkworth?"

"Difficult to tell for sure. Could be a half brother or a cousin. Or maybe no relation at all, though most of Picklescott considers him the vicar's brother. Mrs. Caraway, that's the mother of the dead vicar, brought him along when she married Mr. Caraway, who is also dead." Mathers pulled out a pocket watch and consulted it. "We must make haste, my lord. The ceremony is in less than a half hour."

"Excuse me? What ceremony?"

"The one in which Mrs. Honeywell is to wed Albert Parkworth. Mrs. Caraway had the banns posted before they even took her from London. She may have even bribed a vicar. I believe it is because of the farm belonging to..." Mathers looked upward as if thinking. "I'm sorry, my lord. I'm not sure what to call her. She isn't Mrs. Honeywell, as that was her grandmother. It will be confusing if—"

"Oleana," Jason said. "You may refer to her as Oleana." He felt ill at the news of Oleana, his Oleana, marrying another man. "She's to wed Albert Parkworth?"

A sympathetic look flashed briefly across his secretary's face. "My lord, I believe it is only because of the farm. Or more correctly, the land. The farm was never really profitable, barely enough to provide for Oleana and her parents. Her father resorted to breeding pigs."

"Then why? Why would they want it?"

Mathers consulted his watch again. "We really should get to the vicarage, my lord."

Jason nodded and stood. He and Mathers jogged down the stairs, shouting to the young stable boy to bring their horses. "Go on, Mathers."

"Oleana's parents were far from wealthy. When her father died, the property went to rot because no one would buy the farm. The ground apparently is not—"

Jason held up his hand. "Spare me the specifics of why no one considered the farm to be valuable. I want to know why Albert

Parkworth is desperate enough to marry Oleana for it."

Jason didn't believe for one second Oleana wanted to wed Parkworth. He'd questioned the two footmen, who under strict orders from Wilbert, had put her in the carriage with Parkworth. She'd fought. Screamed that Parkworth was lying.

Begged for someone to find Jason.

A wash of guilt hit him as he tapped his foot, waiting for the stable hand to reappear. Instead of stopping Oleana from being taken, Jason had been entertaining Miss Langham and her mother. Sipping tea while she was forcibly shoved into a carriage.

If the boy didn't appear with his horse, Jason would saddle the damned animal himself.

"According to Mr. Jenkins, who runs the Crowing Rooster down the street—" At Jason's look, he clarified, "The local pub. The farm is important to Mr. Hughes of the Northern Railway. Hughes arrived in Picklescott with a crew of surveyors earlier this year. The surveyors determined that the best, most efficient way to lay their track was smack in the middle of Oleana's farm. Which is now worth a bloody fortune, begging your pardon, my lord."

"How much exactly?"

Mathers named the amount. It was enormous. Even to Jason, whose own holdings brought him a vast amount of wealth. A fortune such as Hughes promised would induce even the most honorable of people to do all sorts of horrible things to gain it.

Like kidnap the widow of a vicar and force her to marry against her will.

The boy appeared with their horses, and Mathers flipped him a coin.

"Oleana was an only child. No other family in the area," Mathers said, turning his horse in the direction of what Jason hoped was the vicarage. "No one else has claim to the property but her. Mr. Hughes didn't arrive to inquire about the land until Percival Caraway was almost six months in the ground. Oleana had been seen out at the old farm and asking around Picklescott what repairs would be needed before she could take up residence there once again because she was no longer welcome in her mother-in-law's home. The general consensus was Mrs. Caraway wanted Oleana gone because she suspected her of frightening the vicar off his horse. In either case, it appears Mrs. Caraway couldn't have cared less before Hughes what became of Oleana or the farm."

"Oleana wouldn't survive five minutes in the dark without tripping over a tree root or a rock, even if she'd wanted to harm the vicar, which I'm certain she did not."

"I agree, my lord. Mrs. Caraway's opinion of her son's widow was well known. Which was what struck Mr. Jenkins as odd when he heard the rumor Oleana was going to wed Albert Parkworth. Very soon after, Oleana vanished into thin air. Albert and Mrs. Caraway were seen digging through what was left of the house at the farm. Rumors started circulating that Oleana is teched in the head. That she's something of a light-skirts and possibly harmed the vicar. Mrs. Caraway also claimed Oleana committed theft, though has never been clear on what was stolen. Most of the people around here assume she took something from the vicarage."

It was apparent to Jason what was happening, and probably clear to Mathers as well. "Mrs. Caraway wants the farm so she can sell it to Hughes." There had never been any theft. Oleana had done nothing criminal. The worst crime she'd committed had been to use a letter of recommendation written for her grandmother, so she could escape the machinations of Mrs. Caraway. "We have to hurry, Mathers. I can't let her wed Albert Parkworth."

"No, my lord. She's your housekeeper, after all."

Jason looked at Mathers, hearing the sardonic tone, but his secretary's face remained impassive. "No. She can't wed Parkworth because she'll be marrying me, Mathers."

Mathers cleared his throat, nudging his horse forward. "I assumed as much, my lord. I should tell you the vicar is a mite uncomfortable about performing the ceremony, despite being told to do so by the bishop and Lord Delacorte. Mrs. Caraway and Lord Delacorte are quite close."

Delacorte. Jason couldn't wait to get his hands on the man who'd obviously aided Mrs. Caraway in her plans. "How do you know all this, Mathers?"

His secretary colored slightly as the vicarage came into view. "I made the acquaintance of the vicar's daughter. She's been very helpful."

Ever resourceful, that was Mathers. Jason planned to give him a raise once Oleana was rescued from this farce of a wedding.

CHAPTER TWENTY

"I'LL ALLOW YOU a bit of ham if you tell me where the deed is, Oleana. The outcome will be the same regardless, but at least you won't go to your wedding hungry."

Oleana declined to look at Mrs. Caraway, deciding to save all the strength she had to escape once they brought her inside the church. Mrs. Caraway had refused to allow Oleana any food until the marriage was finalized. She'd been given only a cup of water each day but no food until this morning, when a watery bowl of oatmeal had been shoved in Oleana's direction. Barely more than a few spoonsful. Light-headed and dizzy, Oleana had made no protest as a stoic-looking woman with a large mole on her chin arrived to dress her for the ceremony.

Mrs. Caraway bit into a slice of ham, chewing slowly while Oleana's mouth watered. The oatmeal hadn't been nearly enough. Oleana's nuptials were in less than an hour, and the best plan she had come up with was to try to escape at the church while the vicar was performing the service. Mrs. Caraway and Albert could hardly bring her before witnesses with her wrists bound.

"Deed?" she whispered. "I'm not sure what you mean. Besides"—Oleana picked at the twine around her wrists—"it was my understanding you didn't need to have that bit of paper. You were going to use your powers of persuasion on Mr. Hughes." Oleana shook her head slightly as the table grew fuzzy before her.

Focus, Oleana.

She would have only seconds to beg the vicar for help. She meant to invoke Montieth's name. Strongly. If that didn't work to stop the ceremony, Oleana would punch Albert in the nose and run for it. Hopefully, the vicar would then be suspicious enough to at least delay the marriage until he could contact the Earl of Montieth.

Mrs. Caraway's lips pursed in displeasure. "My dear, your life will be exceptionally difficult after you marry Albert, I'm afraid. I will enjoy watching you stripped and thrown into a cell, for your own good, of course. You'll never see the light of day, Oleana."

"You promised, Mother, I'd get to enjoy her for a bit first," Albert said.

Oleana swayed in her chair, whether from the thought of being intimate with Albert or because of her weakened state, she wasn't sure. Albert had taken full advantage of her imprisonment, groping and pressing wet kisses on Oleana every time he came to her room with her lone cup of water. Yesterday he'd deliberately dumped the cup on the floor, watching in delight as she'd licked it from the floorboards.

"Of course you will." Mrs. Caraway patted his hand. "I did promise. But then off she goes. I've already sent a letter to Mr. Hughes. He should be arriving at the end of the week. Deed or no deed, we are selling to him as soon as I can arrange it. You can have her until then."

Albert grunted and shoved a mouthful of eggs into his mouth.

"Once wed, you selfish, stubborn girl, you'll go back to your room. After a blissful wedding night, Albert will return to London to collect your things. I'm certain what we're looking for is there and that the butler is too stupid to have found it. Lest you think anyone in London might come for you, I've already written Lord Montieth a pointed letter explaining how ill you are and apologizing for any trouble you may have caused."

"With all my deceit, it is a wonder you want me to marry Albert." The words felt heavy and thick on her tongue. "I'm sure more people will wonder once you come into a large sum of money after selling my farm."

"Charity and forgiveness are what I plan to tell everyone." Mrs. Caraway viciously speared a bit of ham. "Just as Percival would have wanted, I'll say. He loved you so dearly, red-haired whore that you are, and wanted you only to be cared for."

Albert grunted again and took another mouthful of eggs.

"Besides, once we have the money and you're tucked away in Leeds, Albert and I are off to the Continent. I've always wanted to enjoy the delights of Paris." Mrs. Caraway stood and peered across the table at Oleana. "You won't be able to stop us. Nor do I think you'll put up much of a fight today." She stood and made her way to Oleana. "You might have given her too much, Albert." She took ahold of Oleana's chin. "No matter. As long as she's standing, Vicar Thompson will wed you."

Oleana blinked at the sight of two Mrs. Caraways. One of those terrible women was quite enough.

I'll go get my things, shall I?" Mrs. Caraway gave Albert a meaningful look. "Meet me outside with the carriage."

CHAPTER TWENTY-ONE

T HE VICARAGE WAS a lovely building of brown stone, covered in layers of ivy. Just across the way stood a small church shaded by a large elm tree. A plot of land next to the church held neat rows of headstones. Wildflowers sprouted in bursts around the church and courtyard.

Oleana had always loved the view of the church and vicarage. It was what had initially drawn her to Percival, the idea that she could spend a quiet life here helping the people she called her friends. The sight warmed her heart, though there was a light haze over everything. She blinked again. It felt like she was in some sort of a dream.

Focus, Oleana.

She was trying. Honestly, she was. But her limbs felt weighed down, and she'd been clumsier than usual getting into the coach. Thoughts came and went. She couldn't seem to concentrate on the task at hand.

What was the task? Oh, right. Escaping Albert.

Albert untied her wrists as the carriage came to a stop outside the church. "Don't try anything, Oleana, though I doubt you can. Don't worry, it'll wear off shortly after the wedding. You'll enjoy our wedding night. I promise." Albert took hold of her elbow and led her slowly toward the church. She only tripped twice, once on her skirts and the other time because a pebble rolled beneath her slipper.

Albert jerked her upright. "Smile, Oleana. Today's your wedding day."

⫸⫷

JASON LEAPED OFF his horse, not bothering to wait for Mathers. Oleana was inside. A carriage sat outside the vicarage, the driver sitting calmly atop. The man barely glanced at him and Mathers as they strode up the steps to the church. Jason touched the handle of the door, meaning to fling it open, but Mathers placed a hand on his arm, halting him.

"My lord. We are dealing with desperate people. We do not know who is inside or if they are armed. Perhaps it is best we don't announce our arrival lest they become more desperate. There is the vicar and his daughter to consider as well as Oleana."

Jason took a deep breath, composing himself. The pistol in his coat rubbed against his chest in reassurance. He jerked his chin in agreement.

One way or another, Oleana was leaving this church with him.

⫸⫷

OLEANA'S KNEES QUAKED as the vicar droned on about the joining of two souls.

That's what it feels like with Jason.

She slid to the side, and Albert grabbed her, halting the ceremony once more. The vicar had stopped speaking two other times, suggesting the bride looked ill. But after Mrs. Caraway had insisted, reminding him Lord Delacorte, the vicar's patron, as well as the bishop had given their permission, the vicar, flustered, had continued.

The vicar's daughter, whose name Oleana forgot as soon as they were introduced, stood next to Oleana, acting as bridesmaid.

The girl kept shooting her concerned looks.

The vicar looked down at Oleana, his kind, worried face blurred at the edges. She had been standing here thinking how lovely the church was and how everything the vicar said reminded her of the way she felt about Jason, when Albert pinched her viciously.

"Stand up," he hissed.

Albert. Dear God. She was marrying Albert.

Oleana shook her head, trying to dispel the cobwebs. Taking a step back, struggling to get him to release her hand, she whispered, "No."

"Oleana," Mrs. Caraway said in warning.

"No," she said, looking directly up at the vicar, blinking until she saw only one of him. "Absolutely not. I will not take this man. Or this wedding." Her words grew louder. "Or her as a mother-in-law." She waved her bouquet at Mrs. Caraway. "She's horrible."

The vicar stopped immediately. "I think it best if we pause the ceremony. It appears the bride hasn't given her consent to marrying Mr. Parkworth as I was led to believe."

"Continue, vicar," Mrs. Caraway snarled. "She only has cold feet."

The vicar shook his head. "I cannot, in all good faith, do so."

"Wed us, vicar or you'll regret it," Albert said. "Oleana is fine. She's a sot in addition to her other problems."

"I'm not." Oleana looked Albert right in the eye and stomped on his foot. Or at least she assumed she did, because he winced in pain as her heel made contact with his toes. She tossed her bouquet at his head and turned, her hip glancing off a pew as she stumbled down the aisle. If she could just get outside, get away from Albert.

"Oleana, get back here." Albert's voice trailed her. "She's addled, vicar, can't you see?"

"Albert, go after her before she harms herself." Mrs. Caraway's voice echoed in the church.

"I am not," the vicar said in a booming voice, "performing this wedding."

"You will!" Mrs. Caraway yelled back. "Or I will see that you never secure another position anywhere in England."

Oleana fell to the floor, crawling in the direction of the door. If she could just reach the handle, she could pull herself up and open it, run into the trees. If she could just reach it. "Please, vicar." She was sobbing and didn't care. "I don't want to wed him. Please—" She fell to the ground in a blubbering heap just before the door, her fingers clawing at the floor.

A gasp came from the vicar's daughter.

Daisy. Her name is Daisy.

Oleana could hear Daisy rushing toward her as Mrs. Caraway yelled more threats at the vicar.

"Step aside," Albert sneered from behind Oleana.

The vicar's daughter gave a little cry as she was pushed away.

"You troublesome baggage," Albert hissed, grabbing Oleana at the back of the head so he could tug her up by the roots of her hair. "You're only delaying the inevitable. You little—"

The door to the church fell open to reveal two pairs of booted feet. One overly large, huge actually.

I know those boots. Relief filled her, the sort that nearly made her faint.

A grunt met her ears as Albert's hand fell away, followed by the rest of him. There was a thud, then the sound of a fist smacking into flesh. Oleana kept her face pressed to the floor, unable to move, afraid if she did, she'd only fall again.

"Oleana. Sweetheart." Warmth enveloped her. The smells of pine and spicy shaving soap assailed her nostrils.

"I'm dreaming," she whispered into the floor.

"No, my love. You are not." Hands, big and broad, wrapped around her shoulders and pulled her into the safety of a warm chest. "I'm here now."

"Jason." She sobbed into his coat as his fingers threaded gently through her hair, which was falling loose of its pins.

Skirts rustled in agitation behind Oleana. A snarl like that of a cornered animal sounded in the confines of the church. "How dare you interrupt my son's wedding. Who do you think you are?"

Oleana cringed from Mrs. Caraway's voice, curling herself more fully into Jason. He was here. He'd come for her. She laid her cheek against his chest, listening to his heart. He was real.

"I am the Earl of Montieth," Jason boomed, voice dripping with disdain. "And this woman is Oleana Caraway, my former housekeeper and the future Countess of Montieth."

CHAPTER TWENTY-TWO

T HE SCREAMING OF Mrs. Caraway was something to behold. The volume alone was enough to wake the dead in the adjoining cemetery, especially after the constable arrived. Then she wailed like a banshee, begging that Lord Delacorte be summoned. Alas, Mrs. Caraway found no help from that quarter either. He denied any knowledge of Mrs. Caraway's true plans, only admitting he had helped her financially since the death of her son.

Jason didn't believe a word of it, but he let the matter rest for now. As he did with Vicar Thompson, who seemed deeply upset at his part in this farce. He *had* stopped the ceremony, which was enough for Jason to keep from taking further steps.

Parkworth escaped being beaten to a bloody pulp by the intervention of Mathers.

Oleana shivered in Jason's arms, and he pulled her closer, brushing a lock of copper-colored hair from her cheek. Her pupils were dilated. That along with her sluggish movements told Jason she'd been drugged. Probably a dose of laudanum, something to keep her from questioning the entire situation too closely.

Jason lifted her into his arms, carrying her outside while Mathers dealt with the constable. He strode to a clearing on the other side of the church, far enough away that she wouldn't hear or see Mrs. Caraway and her son being carted away. Parkworth was already decrying his part in Oleana's misery, claiming everything had been Mrs. Caraway's idea.

Oleana clung to Jason as if terrified he would disappear. "Jason, you came for me," she whispered in a tone that broke his heart. He knew some of it was the effect of the drug still in her system, but what remained was disbelief.

"Of course I did. You left Carrot. I had to hunt you down for that reason alone. Chastise you—" He kissed the top of her head. "—for the amount of orange fur in my study."

"Wilbert didn't hurt him?" She looked up at Jason with wide eyes.

"No," he assured her. "Carrot is likely, at this moment, sitting on my desk cleaning himself. And Wilbert is gone. I fired him when I found out what happened." His arms tightened around her. Now was not the time, with her thoughts still muddled, to discuss their future. She was still shaking, in shock over what had nearly happened.

"You did not have to go to such great lengths for me, nor lie in front of the vicar," she said quietly.

"Yes, I did. And I told the vicar no lies, Oleana. I want to marry you."

She looked away from him, fingers still clinging to his coat. "You don't mean that, Jason. Think of the scandal. Your mother will not approve. I am nothing more than a farmer's daughter once wed to a vicar. The most I could be is your mistress."

Jason's heart twisted painfully. She was right on all counts, but it didn't matter to him. There had been plenty of time to consider Huntly's advice, which Jason planned to heed. His happiness and that of his daughter far outweighed any scandal that might erupt at his wedding Oleana. He'd known even while reading the letter from Mathers.

"I think it's my decision what you are or aren't to me, don't you? In case you've forgotten, I'm an earl, a very prestigious one from an ancient family. I can do as I please."

"Arrogant," she said, sounding more like herself, "is what you mean."

"Exactly. You can't be my mistress because that would require we live apart, which isn't going to work. Think of Elizabeth. Who will moon bathe with her? And me. I've a very large bed that you've yet to see. Besides, you've finally found the linen closet, according to rumor."

A weak smile crossed her lips. "I'm so sorry for lying to you. But I was desperate to hide from Mrs. Caraway and—" She paused and bit her lip.

"Do you love me, Oleana?" He'd never asked a woman such a thing before, nor had he ever cared how one would answer. He waited several heartbeats, feeling the sting of her silence.

A tear ran down her cheek. "There is something else I must tell you, Jason. I want no more unsaid between us." She plucked at her skirts. "I was unable to conceive when wed to Percival." A sob came from her as she struggled to get up. "I'm useless. Barren."

"You are not useless to me." His voice broke.

She shook her head as more tears fell. "You need an heir. I can't give you one."

"Answer the question, Oleana. Do you love me?"

She sucked in a deep, shaky breath. "Of course I love you." Her shoulders slumped in defeat. "Which is why I *can't* marry you."

"That is unacceptable," he finally said. Logically, Jason had known this would likely be the case. She had been wed for some time and had no children. He thought about what things would be like without an heir for the earldom and found he didn't care. What mattered most was how desolate his existence would be without Oleana. Yes, Jason would have an heir if he gave her up, but he wouldn't have *her*.

She wiped the tears from her eyes. "What do you mean, unacceptable? There isn't anything to be done about it. You must accept it."

"I can't give up Carrot. He's an earl's cat now. If I must wed you to keep him, I shall." He reached for her.

"But—"

"You love me." He brushed his lips with hers. "And I love you." Jason kissed her gently. "I don't need an heir. I just need you."

EPILOGUE

"OLEANA." JASON LOOMED over her as she tugged at another weed, threatening to ruin the calm of the kitchen garden. "I thought you were going to allow the maids to do that."

She sat back on her heels and looked up at her austere, mildly terrifying husband. "How did you know I was out here, my lord?" Berriman, their new butler, had promised not to tell Jason she'd snuck out to work in the garden. The entire household was conspiring against her, it seemed.

"I saw you from the bloody window."

"There isn't any reason to curse." She flopped over, trying to raise herself to her feet, and failed. She was far too large to move about without some help. Knowing her propensity for running into things, she supposed she was fortunate Jason didn't have her padded with pillows as she went about the house. He was terribly overprotective.

"You can't even get up. You are more likely to roll away from me."

Annoyed. Not unusual. "Will you help me?" She took his hand as he lifted her to her feet.

Jason immediately wrapped his arms about her rounded form, pressing a kiss to her temple. "I'm forever terrified you'd fall on the rake or trip into the fountain."

Oleana giggled. "I'm very careful, my lord." She patted her stomach.

The news that she was with child had struck Oleana dumb, coming as it did a mere few months after she and Jason were wed. It had her reconsidering a great many things about her previous life, one of which was that perhaps she hadn't conceived because of Percival. Maybe she had never been barren but had only had the wrong husband.

The idea that Montieth may shortly have an heir even had Lady Trent warming up to her. Somewhat. Jason's mother still found her son's choice of Oleana to be horrifying, to say the least.

Lady Trent's opinion of Oleana was not unexpected. But Mrs. Caraway had been a much more difficult mother-in-law, one who was even now sitting in a place far worse than the sanatorium in Leeds. Mrs. Caraway had been deemed insane. Not even Lord Delacorte could save her. Or Albert. He'd been sent to Australia for his part in her schemes.

Oleana took her husband's hand and placed it over her stomach where a foot was protruding. Dr. Higgans was concerned at how large she'd become and the positioning of the various limbs inside her womb. He suspected twins. "See, everything is fine."

Jason leaned down and brushed a piece of dirt from her cheek, kissing her softly on the mouth. "No more gardening."

Oleana sighed. It was a small concession. He would only badger her until she conceded. At any rate, her lower back had been bothering her all day. "Agreed."

A loud yowl sounded. The row of hedges wiggled violently before parting to reveal Carrot.

"Mousing again?" Jason raised a brow at the large orange cat lumbering in their direction.

"He's trying," Oleana answered. "That counts for something. We must continue to be encouraging."

The large cat wedged himself between Oleana and her husband, wrapping his tail around her ankles, purring wildly.

"Don't worry, Carrot. You'll get that mouse next time."

About the Author

Kathleen Ayers is the bestselling author of steamy Regency and Victorian romance. She's been a hopeful romantic and romance reader since buying Sweet Savage Love at a garage sale when she was fourteen while her mother was busy looking at antique animal planters. She has a weakness for tortured, witty alpha males who can't help falling for intelligent, sassy heroines.

A Texas transplant (from Pennsylvania) Kathleen spends most of her summers attempting to grow tomatoes (a wasted effort) and floating in her backyard pool with her two dogs, husband and son. When not writing she likes to visit her "happy place" (Newport, RI.), wine bars, make homemade pizza on the grill, and perfect her charcuterie board skills. Visit her at www.kathleenayers.com.